WINNERS OF A NATIONAL BOOKSELLERS WRITING CONTEST

The Answer, My Friend

And Other Short Stories
by the People Who Sell Them

MICK BRADY • KATHY CONNER • THOMAS COONEY • BILL COTTER
HONORE HILLMAN FOSTER • CHRISTOPHER HAWTHORNE
KATHRYN LACEY • NANCY ORLANDO
NICOLE REYNOLDS • DONNA STUART

Foreword by Mary Higgins Clark

LONGMEADOW
P R E S S

Published by Longmeadow Press, 201 High Ridge Road,
Stamford, CT 06904.

Cover design by Kelvin P. Oden
Interior design by Donna R. Miller
Cover Photo by Cynthia Danza

Library of Congress Cataloging-in-Publication Data

The answer my friend : and other stories by people who sell them /
    Mick Brady . . . [et al.]. — 1st ed.
        p.   cm.
    ISBN 0-681-00432-0 :
    1. Short stories, American.   I. Brady, Mick.
PS648.S5A6   1994
813' .0108—dc20   93-46516
                                                       CIP

Printed in United States of America
First Edition
0 9 8 7 6 5 4 3 2 1

Contents

Foreword

Publishing lore has it that once upon a time an editor in a foreign land sent this letter to the authors of all unsolicited manuscripts:

We have read your manuscript with boundless delight. If we were to publish your paper, it would be impossible for us to publish any work of a lower standard. And as it is unthinkable that in the next 1,000 years, we shall see its equal, we are, to our regret, compelled to return your divine composition and beg you a thousand times to overlook our short sight and timidity.

It's always a blow to receive a rejection slip. Believe me, I know. My first short story was sold *six years* after I sent it out for the first time. I'd gathered forty rejection slips before that magical day when instead of finding my stamped self-addressed envelope back in my mailbox, I discovered a letter from the editor of *Extension Magazine* with an offer of one hundred dollars for "Stowaway."

But in my files I still have comments like, "Mrs. Clark, your stories are light, slight and trite." Another particularly cutting response was, "We found the heroine as boring as her husband had."

That's why it is such a pleasure to share with all the writers in this volume the particular joy of seeing that first short story in print. I can understand how they felt when the acceptance came. Terrific! Excited! Great!

For some, this may be the one shot at fiction and fame. It was fun but inspired no desire to repeat the experience. For others, it may launch an avocation if not a fulfledged career. In any case, writing always satisfies a deep, inner need for professionals, as well as amateurs. All these stories are fictitious, but all writers surely bring to fiction their own experiences and observations of the experiences of others, their own emotions or emotions they have perceived, and their own backgrounds or the intriguing backgrounds of others.

The short story is a particular art form. It is short. It is a story. The discipline of the short story form means that every word must help the plot to unfold, the tale to be told. There's a wonderful anecdote about the man who wrote to his friend, "I didn't have time to write you a short letter so I'm writing you a long one." All that is tangential or irrelevant or self-indulgent must be vanquished with the delete key.

On the occasion of being honored by the Mystery Writers of America, Isaac Bashevis Singer said, "I do not care how eloquent your phrases, how polished your prose, unless you are a storyteller, you are not a writer. In medieval times the storyteller went from castle to castle. He began with the magical words, 'Once upon a time,' and immediately the room grew quiet and everyone drew closer to the fire to listen. I beg you, begin your stories with those words."

As you read the following pages, I know you will realize that all the contributors understood that writing is truly storytelling. Enjoy the next few hours of reading pleasure.

Once again, I offer my congratulations to all who participated in *The Answer My Friend: And Other Stories . . . By People Who Sell Them*. For those of you who desire to continue writing, I offer, in addition, this bit of advice. When the page is blank, the plot isn't working, the characters are dull, and you're sure that even if you finish the effort, no one will want to read it, two wonderful words have a way of egging you on:

"Royalty Checks."

Mary Higgins Clark
New York
February 1994

The Answer,
My Friend

by Kathryn Lacey

Their faces were webbed with new lines. Although something about their eyes looked
tired, they were still wide open and starry as ever.
Groomed to a shine, Peter, Paul, and Mary stood
on the stage. Much like the baby-boomers watching, they were thicker, balder, and less natural than
they used to be. And like the boomers watching,
something was lost; the crisp golden harmony
now fell lower, raspier, and rang more reminiscent
than revolutionary.

From the audience, Crystal watched the three hover around their microphones on the large stage, the Cincinnati Philharmonic stage right and a large choir stage left. Under bright illumination, the stage seemed bloated as the robed choir reverberated an operatic refrain of "Blowing in the Wind." The pristine harmony was as beautiful as it was painful for Crystal to hear. It was some kind of revision of history. Crystal had to look away.

She noticed her comrades of the evening in the balcony, swallowed in rows and rows of plush red seats. Forty bucks a head nodded to the pacifying strings. Peter, Paul, and Mary were trying to transport them back, and that's what bothered Crystal. She wasn't one who liked to look back. Hearing them, it was too easy to pretend to be Back Then. With her eyes closed, she could again feel the prick of a grassy knoll. She could again be a reclining body among thousands in various stages of undress, feeling a part of the same body, taking a smoking joint from a stranger and hearing that perfectly sweet harmony flow over her like warm water. Back Then, a little of the outrage was set to three parts and an acoustic guitar. It was not so pristine and operatic. It had been a little out of tune, Back Then, though no one remembered that way.

Crystal preferred to open her eyes and to see the receding hairlines and the thickening midriffs of those around her. She had felt like a walking stereotype then and felt twice as generic now. Crystal could feel the nostalgia fad creep up on her. It was set to music, perfectly scored and orchestrated.

Her daughter, Amber, sat beside her, squinting at the three singers. During the a cappella rendition of "Early Morning Rain," Crystal had looked to see her closed eyes and nodding head, as pacified as her fellow audience members by the "trip." The woman in front of Amber placed her newly done hair on the shoulder of the gentleman next to her. In fact, many heads were nodding. But no one was smoking a joint. Maybe no one would even admit they had inhaled. That seemed to be popular with the election and all. But the person Crystal used to be had. The person Crystal was trying to leave behind had done it all.

Her attention back on the stage, she counted how many of the choir were actually over twenty-five. Very few. They stood erect and still. Their mouths formed perfect O's to articulate just the right sound. It was like hearing Jimi Hendrix Muzak, Crystal decided. "Purple Haze" on the organ.

"They're pretty cool," Amber said. Her white-blond hair bounced around her shoulders in waves. Her twenty-year-old eyes sparkled even in the dim houselights. She was the image of Crystal. They both had the same heart-shaped face, the same lapis eyes. They shared a petite build, though Crystal worked at it these days in premenopause aerobic torture. The glaring difference between mother and daughter was that Amber had bleached her "to-die-for-Katherine-Hepburn hair" to be Madonna or Marilyn. Even so, Crystal was relieved to see a contrast between the two of them.

It mocked her less.

"Yeah, well, they used to be cool," Crystal said. Someone down front lit a Bic lighter and held it up as their signature song faded out.

This made Crystal wonder if they ever realized the moment the magical decade of the sixties had ended: New Year's Eve 1969? Kent State? Maybe as late as '75, when the war finally ended, the draft dodgers pardoned, and abortion was legalized? For Crystal, perhaps, Amber had signaled the end of that era. It was as welcome a change for Crystal as it was unwelcome. But looking around her, now and at work, she could see some people had not abandoned it all so easily.

The last war song sounded, the last magic dragon puffed away. Crystal and Amber filed out quietly with the smiling, satiated crowd. Amber slipped her arm around her mother. She was going through a weird touching stage lately.

"That was pretty awesome," Amber said. "Don't know if I'll tell my friends, though. They don't really get how cool it all was. I mean, some of them do. Like Betsy listens to Eric Clapton and stuff. She'd appreciate it."

"Glad you enjoyed it," Crystal said.

"Her mom just bought this big book by Paul McCartney's wife about the sixties. I told her that you'd probably think it was cool."

There were things Crystal did not do anymore, now that she was a management consultant, pushing forty-three. One was to look at old photos of her heyday. The whole popularity of the Decade of Hip had been captured in that amazingly successful photo album/coffee table book by Linda who still wasn't considered much more than a Beatle's wife. It was hard for Crystal to fathom that her life could be reduced to a montage of photos of hippies in varying degrees of intoxication. It equally astonished her that her daughter could walk into the house in a pair of Birkenstocks and a tie-dyed T-shirt, a huge metal peace sign pounding her tiny chest. People liked to point out these circular trends in fashion and call it further proof of parallel history.

Unlike her peers, however, Crystal didn't make critical leaps of parallelism between the L.A. riots and Kent State, between the Gulf War and the Vietnam War, between Clinton and Kennedy. She didn't buy into these conversations in the pricey lunchroom in the Mead Building, where she did most of her consulting. There they were in their suits and ties, their crisp dress-suits and hose and pumps, trying to find a string of logic to connect to that time, a way of saying: "Ah, yes, this is the place it all leads — this generation must deal with what we already have." She didn't follow this string. They wanted to keep pushing the border of the past until it was not evident when that era had slipped away. They'd rather look back than into a mirror. Crystal preferred looking straight ahead.

"I've seen the book," Crystal said. She pulled Amber around to walk forward. "It's too expensive for a bunch of pictures."

Stepping into the city, Crystal saw the light show of the Mead Building in the distance. The river was sending off a breeze that shifted the humidity like a damp sheet. They walked in silence to the parking garage, passing the shiny black glass of galleries, the redbrick thrift shops, and the washed-out stones of the Chinese restaurant on the corner. Traffic spun by loudly. A boy in slashed-up jeans, black leather jacket, and shaved head cut past them. A young woman in a leather miniskirt and a black lace brassiere followed him. Amber's eyes looked up and down the Madonna wannabe, taking in every detail. Perhaps, Crystal thought, I should have raised her during the early years and left this for someone else. Amber's gum snapped loudly as punctuation.

"Hey, Mom, how come you took me tonight, instead of whatzisname?" Her eyes were now checking out a skinhead leaning against a boutique window. He had a swastika tattooed on his forearm.

"Whatzisname's name is Bill. I thought you might like it. I'm getting a little tired of hearing Iced Tea hip-whatever on your stereo all the time," Crystal said, steering her daughter into the concrete parking garage.

"It's Ice T, Ma. Keep up, willya?" she said. They walked up the ramp. "It's **rap**, not hip-hop, okay?"

"Right. Whatever." They made their way more quickly, footsteps echoing through the garage. The skyline reached up into the dark space of sky, screaming a manic array of lights. She could barely make out the river, rippling darkly beneath the bright Queen City Bridge as it winded its way into Kentucky. They slid into Crystal's silver BMW.

The truth was that Whatzisname Bill was history. He was an investment banker whom Crystal had been less dating and more trying to shake, like a nagging rumble in the chest. He was taken with too many bourbons, which made him sexually excited and impotent at the same time. He was in a typical, post-divorce adolescence—taking sudden interest in loud music, growing his hair long in back to compensate for the thinning top, and swinging from mood to mood like a chimp on steroids.

Bill was a handsome enough man, though. He did the executive workout, as was popular to tame the savage belly and kept his salt and pepper beard trim, as well. Too trimmed, actually, which made Crystal want to grab some clippers and make his jawline a bit ragged. He wore tailored suits and spoke French from the menus. He also followed women with his eyes. Young women. Girls, actually, not much older than Amber. Last week at dinner, that thought had hit her, as Bill poked at his escargots and eyed the babyfaced waitress. A picture in vivid Technicolor came to Crystal of Bill and Amber lying on the couch together, watching MTV. Amber snapping her gum while he said, "Far out." Crystal had decided before the entrée arrived that she was dumping Bill.

"Wow, that harmony was great," Amber said,

settling into the faded leather seat. "So all the music was that mellow then, huh?" Amber twisted a bit to face Crystal. "The big retro movement is happening in music — Indigo Girls, Toad the Wet Sprocket, R.E.M. They're all very cool. The past is making a big comeback."

"I guess it was mellow by today's standards. Some of it was not so mellow, though. Hendrix on the electric guitar. He was—"

"Yeah, he's bad. Bad-good." Amber automatically clarified these things these days. "Jimmy Z listens to him even now."

"Right. Jimmy Z." This was a kid, who in his long-haired lanky way, had startled Crystal. He was Amber's latest boyfriend, dragged home like a stray dog from Ohio State University. He was staying in the city somewhere, maybe in a cardboard box on a street corner. He flashed the peace sign frequently and took particular pride in his lack of hygiene and chain smoking. He often sat motionless, staring at nothing. Lately, he had gotten Crystal thinking about things she never wanted to think about.

"Well, he likes Metallica, too. You know them?" Amber asked.

"Are they the ones who were naked on the cover of *Rolling Stone*?" Crystal gunned her BMW's engine and whipped out of the garage.

"No. That was Red Hot Chili Peppers. Metallica has the lead singer you said looks like Manson," Amber said, running her hand through her crazy hair.

"Ah. You said, if I recall, 'cool.' Is Manson cool these days? According to Jimmy Z?" Crystal couldn't help it. The Z always came out sarcastically. The name sounded like a loan shark in Reno. Earlier in the week, she had come in from the office to find them lying on the couch, stretched out and comfortable in the ways their bodies met. They were in what was called at one time, the spoon position. They were fully dressed, and for some reason, this bothered Crystal even more. They gazed at MTV as if it were an aphrodisiac. Four young black men, well-dressed in suits, were singing a love song in pristine harmony. Crystal was certain there was a sweet lingering odor of pot in the air, taunting her like a ghost.

In the BMW, Amber protested weakly, "Aw, Ma. Give me a break here. Manson is what? seventy? Most people think he's dead. Ancient his-tor-y. And lay off Jimmy Z. You don't understand him. Most people don't. He's had a hard life."

They drove in silence for a while. Crystal concentrated on the traffic. She bit her tongue from saying, "Having neither MTV nor Nintendo can be rough on any kid." Amber was too sensitive. She didn't take sarcasm or criticism well.

"I know you don't like him. You never like any of them," Amber continued. "Remember my boyfriend in high school? Tod, the jock? Mr. Clean-Cut? God, you hated him. Told him before the prom, if he knocked me up you'd blow his brains out!" Amber laughed. "He was too scared to kiss me good night. I mean, what did you do with your boyfriends during the Summer of Love? Arm wrestle?"

This was another thing Crystal did not do— enumerate her past and have it held up as a yardstick.

"What do we get nowadays?" Amber went on. "The Summer of the Eleven O'clock Curfew. We do sit-ins because the school wants to require phys-ed as a liberal-arts requirement. Campus is dry; narcs enroll as students. 'Just say no.' It's intensely uptight. We feel cheated. It was so free and easy then. Kids getting stoned and drunk and having sex without giving a shit about their parents, much less life and death. Everyone was so laid back. These days there's the sense that sex is suicide in one form or another."

Crystal's grip instinctively tightened on the steering wheel. "Amber, there was a war on. Everyone was not 'laid back.' Funny how kids your age, even kids my age, have romanticized the whole idea of the sixties." Crystal thought she could manipulate this conversation to remain political, pragmatic, and informational. She could control it without a stroll down memory lane. "Besides, don't believe everything you hear. Things weren't all that crazy everywhere. Many people lived very normal lives in the sixties."

"Yeah. Yeah. Normal lives. Kids my age have the summer of boredom. Bannerless. Fightless. The no-name Generation X."

"Count your blessings," Crystal said. As she

did, she heard her own mother recounting the hardships of the Depression and women having to work in factories to support their families, which of course wasn't necessary during Vietnam. This was not the way Crystal wanted this conversation to go. She did not want to believe personal histories of mother-daughter discussions could repeat endlessly, generically, forever.

"Did you go to war protests? Fight and get arrested? Did you ever hit a cop? I mean, you were at Kent State then. I tell my friends, 'Yeah, my mom was there during the riots.' And they want to know what you did, but I don't know what to tell them." Crystal could feel the weight of Amber's stare.

Nostalgia for Crystal couldn't be collected and crammed into a shoe box or a safety deposit box. It didn't need to be. In an instant, the sour smell of horse and sweat and gunpowder could be burning in her nostrils. The screaming could cloak her in swirling madness. The infamous Kent State riot had been a jumble of legs and feet, kicking and running and tripping. As she lay on the ground beneath the mass of legs and bodies blurring above her, a careful horse carrying an officer stepped over her, swallowing the sun. She was not shot, not bleeding, just too slow to move. Lying on concrete, shivering, expecting a bullet did not feel so radical, did not feel like history. She knew people, her comrades, who saved and cherished rocks, horseshoes, and spent bullet casings like gold. To remind them.

"I was studying during the riot. I was not a

'flower child,' though I knew people who were. I also knew people who liked to yell and try to change the world. I also knew people who studied, worked to support themselves, were virgins, and probably didn't care about the war or the protests at all." Crystal tried to assume a look of concentrating on the traffic. She didn't want to look at her daughter as she revised her history. How much did Amber really need to know?

"Why didn't you tell me about this stuff?" Amber asked.

Crystal drove in silence as they moved from the city to the trimmed, clean suburbs. Traffic was slowing down, backing up.

"Dad," Amber persisted, "how come you never talk about him?"

It had been a time when nostalgia was old green Coke bottles and crackers that came in tins. At that time, history was poodle skirts and hula hoops and "I Like Ike." Her life then had been quietly going along in a noisy time when Timothy O'Leary's pledglings were eager to drop in, out and acid. Time and nostalgia cruised by her like pink flamingos transforming into ceramic geese. It was a solid time line, a continuum she slid along, not so gracefully as reluctantly and then, indifferently. She was glad to see many of the things slip away and wanted in no way for them to return. Though they always seemed to, like her daughter's peace medallion, bell-bottoms, and exposed navel. It had been hard enough the first time without the pain of déjà vu.

"There's not much to tell, really," Crystal said. "It's not quite as it was cracked up to be. Some of us really did lead quite boring lives." Like a blob of gray-white in the center of psychedelic colors, so he had said, Amber's father, Denny. I'm not going to tell her, Crystal told herself. There's no reason. My daughter's already in the spoon position.

They sat unmoving in the middle of a caravan of strangers all escaping the lights and towers of the city. Amber pulled her body half out of the car window to see over the other cars. From her seat, Crystal could see jumping red and blue lights.

"A monster of a train is half on the track, half turned over on its side." It struck Crystal that there was a morbid excitement growing—if her daughter said, "cool," it was off to the convent for her to study with nuns.

Amber plopped back onto her seat. "Looks like we have to wait," she said. "Maybe it was carrying toxic waste or some deadly chemical."

"Nice, Amber. Very nice," Crystal shut off the engine. "Always hope for the worse. Very healthy." The humidity made the evening air seem thick.

Amber snapped her gum, and Crystal felt her spine tingle a bit in that way mothers' spines do. This made her think for a second, I am a good mother. I have the tingle. She dismissed the thought. She was not into deluding herself.

"Toxic spills happen," Amber said, more to herself than to Crystal.

They were on a two-way thoroughfare that cut

through suburban alcoves with names like Pleasant Farms and Dove's Circle. On either side of the
road were high fences to keep some element out.
Or in, maybe. Crystal's own suburban house was
not more than six miles farther up the road. The
tract houses beyond the fences all looked like her
own. Crystal knew there existed chemically green
grass and perfectly trimmed hedges for privacy.
There were sedans and station wagons, shorter and
more sportier than they used to be, sitting in
Genie-controlled garages. Warm glows flickered
and danced, insinuating the presence of television.
Crystal looked at the bumper of the BMW in front
of hers bearing the sticker: Don't blame me, I voted
for Bush. It was a newer model of BMW than hers.
It was what they called, "less boxy."

Silence was something uncomfortable for her.
In these moments, Crystal thought she should
impart some wisdom to her daughter. Tell her
something useful, motherly. Usually, she had the
urge to apologize. Really, right that moment, all
that came to her were words from Peter, Paul, and
Mary, asking for a head count. How many, indeed,
Crystal wondered.

Amber said, "I picture him as this cool professor at Kent with you. A lot older than you, but
very hip, you know? And married."

"What are you talking about?" Crystal was
thinking hell may be being trapped in a BMW with
a broken radio and a teenager on a mission.

"My father," Amber said. "I'm not pulling an
Orphan Annie or nothing. He's not going to come

in and make us the Huxtables, but I want to know. Until I do, I'll make stuff up. Sometimes he's a folksinger or a draft dodger."

"You're a born romantic, you know that?" Crystal said. "I was inseminated, okay?" She felt a stiffness crawl up her neck.

"Ma," Amber sighed, as Crystal received a light back-handed slap on the arm, "come on."

"Well, I was. The old-fashioned way. Okay. He wasn't a dodger or a professor or a circus freak or a famous rock star. Those are my cheekbones, not Mick Jagger's." They both laughed.

Crystal wondered what threatening conversations were going on in the other vehicles. The middle-aged driver in the new BMW looked out his windows, ignoring a woman speaking into a cellular phone. Farther ahead, two kids crawled out on the hood of their Nova and began making out as if at a drive-in movie. From somewhere, a dull throbbing of a bass pulsated beneath a fast snarl of words.

"Who, then?" Amber began tapping the dash board with her red-painted finger nails. "You always said, we shouldn't keep secrets."

"I never said that!" Crystal jerked around to face Amber. Crystal had never been one of those mothers who read their daughter's diary or have frequent gossip sessions about her kid's sexual exploits. "I like secrets. Secrets save stress and emotional anguish. You must have picked that up in TV land. Secrets are good. No one needs to know everything about each other. Trust me on that. If your father had known that much we'd not be having this conversation."

As soon as Crystal said this and slumped back into her bucket seat, Amber perked up. She put her hand on her mother's arm. Crystal shook it off.

"What does that mean, about Dad?" Amber asked.

"Nothing." Silence lingered, heavy with waiting.

Finally, Crystal said, "He had many habits that would have been better kept a secret, as do most people." The car seemed more cramped. She opened her door to let in some air.

"Like what? Satanic rituals? Bank robberies?" Amber stopped tapping the dash. "What?"

"God, you're so melodramatic." Crystal tried to will the traffic to move.

"It's my age. I'm supposed to be melodramatic. Weren't you?" Again, pulling out the yardstick. Crystal tried to remember ever wanting to know who her mother was as a person or wanting to understand her. Somehow, nothing really came to mind. Crystal saw far too much of her mother as she grew up. Amber couldn't really say that.

"It was the climate, then," Crystal said. "We were saving the world. It's an occasion that calls for melodrama."

"What bad habits? Besides drugs, I mean," Amber persisted. "I mean, I assume dope. But what else? What habits?"

From far off, Crystal said, "Of confusing love and pain."

She was thinking of those old Coke bottles and how the thick, green glass didn't shatter even when racked across her temple. No one collected this sort of nostalgia, and she didn't want her daughter to begin. What Crystal collected was a dim room off Sixth Street in Akron where a tired fat man, reeking of Brylcreem and Old Spice laid her flat on a table and warned that he wasn't liable for this. There was Denny in the corner smoking a Camel, unfiltered, saying, "Just hurry up with it, old man," like the guy was about to fire up a hamburger rather than use dirty instruments to scrape away a mistake growing inside her. Nostalgia was the wave of nausea that rolled through her as she walked away, physically untouched, into the heat of the Summer of Love.

"Guess we're getting hitched," Denny had said, lighting up another Camel from the one he was smoking and handing it to her like a pact being sealed. They stood quietly smoking as they watched two kids in fringed buckskin jackets splatter their VW van with bright paint, all the while giggling in a stoned frenzy. Crystal felt she was drowning in the gray-white blob surrounded by the vivid color of Denny. Sucking deeply on her cigarette, in her silence, she had accepted his proposal.

During the six-week marriage, Crystal lived through the pop bottle concussion, two broken ribs, three black eyes, and a broken ring finger. At least, a part of her lived through it. A part of her crawled back into gray-white center like a wounded soldier.

It was just a matter of timing. Roe v. Wade would change things in a year. It's not that Crystal wasn't glad to have the baby who would evolve into Amber, but sometimes Crystal felt as if there was shrapnel left inside her.

In the BMW, she began humming an off-key version of the chorus of "Blowing in the Wind." A nervous habit.

"What's that mean? Love and pain?" Amber asked. Again, she touched her mother's arm lightly. "He hit you?" The pain was already in her daughter's voice. The betrayal already evident in her eyes.

"No. Of course, he didn't hit me. He wasn't like that. What kind of gene pool do you think I'd choose from? Don't hang on me. It's muggy already." She shifted a little, then pulled the door shut.

"Truth, Mom. I can handle it."

Which truth could she tell? The "I was in a car wreck" truth to explain bruises she had told friends? The "Amber was conceived with a soldier killed in the war" truth she had tried to pass off on her mother, Amber's grandmother, just before dumping the kid off for ten years in Cincinnati? Or maybe the "I didn't do something so stupid as" truth, which she told herself every day. A line from the song continued to circle in her head like a vulture. She had long ago lost count of the number of times she had voluntarily turned her head and pretended not to see anything. Crystal sighed and before she could think about it, she began.

"We met — now, don't get excited — on my way to Woodstock in '69, August. It was the summer before my freshman year at Kent. Mom still lived here, but I had moved to start school." Once she started, Crystal wondered just how much she would tell.

"Cool!" Amber was clearly excited. "You were at Woodstock!"

"Not exactly," Crystal said, shifting position in her seat. "I was one of the thousands of cars stuck in traffic on my way to Yasgur's farm. Bumper to bumper for miles, waiting for rain. No room to turn around for a while, nowhere to go. We couldn't hear the music. Just the helicopters shipping in food and water."

"And you met my father?"

"Sort of. Denny had ridden the same van as me and six others. I think he was my friend Ruthie's boyfriend's cousin's friend. He was older. Twenty-four. Apparently he had been a peace activist at Kent but not enrolled. Anyway, he popped out of the van in these old rollerskates and started rolling up and down between cars. He had a way of making a party out of any occasion. He was giving out or selling joints and hits of acid. I shouldn't be telling you this—" no, she shouldn't. The alarms were going off in shrill unison with the fire truck and ambulance sirens wailing up the road.

"Mother, don't treat me like a child." There was, in fact, nothing in Amber's voice, her face, her high-gloss, red nail polish that resembled a child.

"You never did before."

"Oh, that's a pretty easy shot." Crystal considered walking home from here, tiptoeing around the imaginary toxic waste and the derailed train in her pumps and symphony clothes. But home would do nothing to stop this force of nostalgia washing over her.

"You never have treated me like a child. You told me about sex when I was seven, remember? I was at grandma's—"

"Where I dumped you. Go ahead. Say it."

"I never said that." Amber started chipping off the red nail polish. "But now that you mention it, yeah — dumped me off for ten years and visited bearing knowledge of sex, menstruation, and how to avoid the boys."

"Important knowledge that your grandmother didn't quite have the vocabulary for. Trust me. I know. You needed to know." Crystal wanted to insist she would not be forced to feel bad in her own boxy, luxury sedan. But what did it matter? She felt bad whenever she looked at the stranger in her daughter. Even worse, the stranger who was herself in the throes of the Summer of Love.

"You told me about menopause when I was eight, Mother. I didn't need to know that. I still don't, as a matter of fact." Amber picked voraciously at her nail polish, revealing a fuchsia pink, days old, beneath.

"Am I going to spend the rest of this derailment defending my life to you? Is this what you mean by secrets—why you were abandoned to your grandmother? I've told you, I was in my senior year at Kent and your grandmother took care of you. Then I worked for a while and visited as often as I could, until I could support both of us. End of story."

"No, it's not. There's more to your story. At least I hope there is. I want to understand why you said something to me when I was little. It was worse than the menopause thing. God, I remember it so clearly. More clearly than anything in my childhood. When I cried as you were leaving after your weekly visit and I grabbed for you, you pulled me off, squatted down, and looked me in the eye. You said, 'Child, you love me too much.' Why would you tell a kid that? What makes someone tell another person that? That's the story I want." Amber's face was red. Her eyes watery.

There they were on Crystal, the clutching hands of a toddler, bawling as if walking to slaughter. Nostalgia was the puffy red eyes of the betrayed and her mother, the kindly grandmother, standing in the background, clucking and tutting away. Crystal wasn't so sure it was Amber she had been speaking to when she said those words.

There were days now when Crystal walked through the empty tract house where she herself had grown up, willed to her by her mother, and felt it all again. The furniture still remained from her own single-parent youth—Queen Anne chairs, heavy mahogany tables, the creaking rocking chair. The furniture was as solid and inflexible as her mother had been after her father was killed in the

Korean War.

Sitting in her car, now, it occurred to Crystal that perhaps that's why she kept the old house, to feel endless punishment, to allow her liver to grow back again and again, like Prometheus protecting his secret. She kept it so she could wear pain like a garment protecting and killing her all at once. Crossing over the threshold of that house, Crystal realized, was a crossing of the barriers of space and time.

"Yeah, well, I guess, I'm to blame for the fact that you're attracted to neurotic grunge-monsters," Crystal said. The battle was not between Crystal and Amber, but between what conversation they would or would not have.

"Oh, another easy shot at Jimmy Z. He's too simple a target," Amber said, sighing as if resigned to the fact that Crystal was hopelessly judgmental.

"That's what I mean. You've always gone for the wounded bird, every time. Trouble. Trust me. I do know." She was losing the battle.

"Is that what Dad was? A wounded bird? Or did he just up and cut the mothering instinct right out of you? I mean, really. Love too much? That's lame for a flower child." Amber turned her back to her mother, angry. Any other time, Crystal would have done some yelling herself at her insolent daughter. But she couldn't feel angry at someone who only wanted the truth to make sense.

What Denny had cut out of Crystal was done not with fists or Coke bottles but with words. This was the real lie that could not find truth. "Your

father was the real hippie, not me. I wore beads
and gypsy clothes. I had hair to my ass and a
perpetual buzz. I also had serious intentions in
school and avoided conflict. No easy task in the
sixties, believe me. I'm not the star of 'Hair' or
whatever is giving you these delusions. Your father was a wannabe musician, like every other
young person who had heard the likes of Janis
Joplin. We were convinced anyone with a bad
haircut, a lot of attitude, and a vein full of smack
could sing the blues.

"That day on the road to Woodstock, he got
in my face and told me he didn't like women much.
To him, they were good for one thing—to lick hits
of acid off of and that's it. A real charmer, your dad.
Maybe I took it as a thrown-down gauntlet. We
pandered his goods. We went back to Kent State,
and off and on for four years, we fought and loved.
When I was pregnant with you, I realized what a
mistake he was in my life."

It was a draft of history with a ring of truth,
anyway.

Amber stared into space like Jimmy Z. She
was hurt. Point proven, Crystal wanted to say.
Secrets were not very helpful.

"So why'd you hang with him then. If he was
such a pig?" Amber finally asked.

Here's where the truth and lies didn't con-
verge. It was the part of the montage of photos in
her life of which she could make no sense. Denny
had looked her right in the face on the road to
Yasgur's farm and said, "You don't know how to

love, girl." It was not a statement of her physical abilities. Perhaps it was because she hadn't let him lick acid off her. He'd repeat this sentiment often, and it was a secret she could have lived without knowing. It was the secret she swallowed with each punch from her lover. It was the secret she held in her arms as she held Amber for the first time. Too much, too little. It was all starting to feel the same. She had not wanted history to repeat itself. But maybe it had.

"I don't know, Amber. He wasn't really a pig. He just had these ambitions. Then when I was about six months into you, Denny got a longing to go on the road like Jack Kerouac. Take up the torch. I don't know what happened to him." The last she'd heard, Denny was a real estate agent in California. He had been featured in an architecture magazine, showing off his large house in Bel Air, with his five kids and wife. He was balding, wearing a suit and tie, and round around the middle. As a matter of fact, he was president of the National Realtor's Association. The name he wore now was Denison.

"It doesn't make sense," Amber said. "The love and pain thing. Why you didn't want to tell me. I don't really understand."

"I hope you never do," Crystal said.

"It sounds like you're leaving something out, somewhere," Amber said, distantly. She was staring out the window at the fenced-off suburb.

The traffic began moving slowly. The two kids on top of the Nova crawled back into their car. The woman in the less boxy BMW continued talking on her phone. The man with her shuffled his papers and closed the briefcase on his lap. Crystal started up her car, still feeling the confines of a van on the road to Yasgur's farm.

"If I love too much, it sounds like I got if from you," Amber said to the window. "Like it or not. Even with my limited details and limited experience, I know that much."

"Not so limited," Crystal admitted, patting her daughter's knee.

"Well, I guess I like my romanticized versions better, if you don't mind. There's a lot to be said for romance," Amber said. Maybe romancing the past was the best lie of all, Crystal decided. It was a nostalgia with which they all could live.

They drove slowly past the train wreck where men in shiny silver suits stood like grim statues, smudged and sweaty. A man with a ruddy face impatiently waved them through with a bright flashlight. Crystal looked in her rearview mirror at the smoking, twisted train, watching it shrink behind them. Transposed over the view were the words, "Objects reflected are closer than they appear."

Amber turned around in her seat to get another look.

"No dead people lying around," Amber announced, feigning, Crystal hoped, disappointment.

"Only survivors," Crystal added, almost to herself. She looked in the mirror, just to be sure.

Going West

by Mick Brady

I was sitting on the side of U.S. 24, which is a little piece of crap road that connects towns with names like Chinquapin and Duplin and Peytona, and I was trying hard to rub my backside into the rusty ground so my white shorts would just look dirty instead of menstrually stained, which they were. I would have been chewing on a grass stem, except all the grass was dead.

All our clothes were dirty, and probably mildewing, in black plastic garbage bags in the back

of the van. I could have got a pair of used underwear and dark shorts to solve my immediate problem, but the back doors didn't open so I would've
had to climb into the van, and Mel would have a
fit if I did that because he had it jacked up, and
my weight might cause the whole damn thing to
fall down on him, which at that particular moment
I didn't care if it did.

Mel was trying to get the spare tire out from
under the van. It was blocked by the twisted
bumper—a result of the same accident that kept
the rear doors from opening. We hadn't got it fixed
because we couldn't report it to the insurance after the other two accidents, one of which wasn't
even Mel's fault. The same was true of the crushed
panel door. It was held on to the van with a cord
tied to the middle bench seat. Mel had covered the
gaping window with a plastic blue tarpaulin that
flapped like crazy on the highway. I told him it
made the van look like a gypsy wagon, but he said
it was protection from the rain. It worked great—
it was protecting the entire Southeast.

Mel wasn't getting anywhere. I could tell,
because he was saying "Jesus fucking Christ" over
and over in an Australian accent that was steadily
getting worse. I couldn't blame him. It was damn
hot. I was starting to feel sticky and gritty between
my legs instead of just sticky, and sweat was cas-
cading down my midriff.

Some chick on the radio was singing about
how all she wanted in life was a bed that wouldn't
hurt her back and a pen that wouldn't run out of

ink and a bunch of other insipid stuff. "Shouldn't I have this?" she whined. And then, sounding like what I imagine—never having heard one—a sick heifer would sound like, "passionate kisses, passionate kisses, wo-oo-wo, passionate kisses from you." If I'd had a gun in my pocket, I would have shot out the radio just to shut her up.

Before I knew I was hearing a different sound, I glanced down the road toward the west. Sure enough, in the shimmering high noon heat waves rising from the asphalt, a semi appeared. It was like seeing a ship on the horizon, or an oasis in the desert. Trucks have tools, I thought. The semi grew into its true imposing bulk as I stood up, waving my arms frantically and doing a kind of jitterbug that I hoped would convey dire need. Suddenly the semi's sound struck, and all at once it was loud and fast and I swear the sonuvabitch not only did not slow down, he leaned into the accelerator a little as he passed us, sending a big whoosh of dust right into my face. My throat reacted first. A persistent tickle at the back turned into an irritating, strangulating sort of feeling and then I was coughing and trying to inhale at the same time. Then I had a sneezing fit. We're talking hurricane force, no ladylike *achoos*. Reflexively, I reached up and rubbed my eyes. Oh hell, I thought immediately. I blinked. The left one was still there, but I had rubbed my right contact out of my eye. I looked at the ground near my feet as though my lost lens would be shining up at me like a bright penny, but all I saw was settling dust and brown weeds.

I have to be honest. I really hate it when people cry the way I did on the side of U.S. 24 that day. It was totally ugly, out-of-control, heaving bawling, right up there with having a baby or real bad diarrhea. It just *had* to come out. And when it did, my lips were all stretched around my teeth, and my legs were shaking in their dirty, bloody shorts, and sweat and dust and tears were all running into my mouth while saliva was running out, and I knew in a detached way that my eyes were probably an attractive shade of green just then but would be all bloodshot in a moment—it was that sort of crying.

Mel got out from under the van and put his arms around me, adding grease to the rest of the crud on my skin. He smelled like B.O., and when he crooned "No worries, mate" for about the ninth time, I had a vision of the future in which he had a broken nose caused by my trembling little fist.

Mel isn't really Australian, and his name isn't really Mel. It's Danny, which is a name I like quite a bit better, by the way. We met in the drama department at Eleanor Roosevelt College, which is an artsy little private school "nestled in the beautiful Blue Ridge Mountains of western North Carolina" where rich Democrats send their kids. I was Kate to Mel's Petruchio, and everyone agreed that our chemistry was terrific.

Danny changed his name to Mel after our trip to Australia. That was the summer after we graduated—we used the money my parents had given me to buy a car. I figured it was my present, but they were extremely indignant about it. Mother: Real life is not just fun and games. Daddy: You've got to start behaving like a responsible adult. Mother: We're not going to be around to take care of you forever. Daddy: It's time to stop dreaming and think about your future.

They ended up telling me to call home for a bus ticket when I got my head screwed on straight. They said if I wanted to follow "that guy" around on his adolescent escapades they were not going to pick up the tab. Jeez—you'd think I'd blown their last ten thousand dollars.

The Australia trip was not an adolescent escapade. It was an adventure. For example, we saw *Rigoletto* at the Sydney Opera House. (That's the building that looks like it has wings that they always show on "Wheel of Fortune" when the prize is a trip to Australia.) When we were in Cairns, we sailed on the *Ocean Spirit* to this little island called Michaelmas Cay. The Northern Territory was the best. We went on a bus tour into Kakadu National Park and saw crocodiles and kangaroos and real aborigines. Fairdinkum. (That's Australian for "no shit.")

Another thing that's fairdinkum is what happened at LAX on our way home. We distinctly heard a girl say, "Was that Mel Gibson?" as we walked out of a gift shop. Danny had been practicing his new Australian accent with the clerk, but he really does kind of look like him, too. So I started calling him Mel for a joke, and that's how he got his new name. And that's when he started calling

me Gert. My real name is Gertrude, but everyone
calls me Trudy except for Danny. I mean Mel.

After the trip we were pretty much out of
money and ideas, and I only had two weeks left
on my lease, when Mel just popped up one day
with what he called our "new regime." It was a
June morning and the coffeemaker was bubbling
away. I was busy copying pickle recipes my mother
had sent onto looseleaf sheets with plastic protec-
tors. Mel said, "We're going to the coast." I remember distinctly that he walked into the room wearing only jeans, drying his hair with one of my
kitchen towels, which always annoyed me, and
climbed up on the chair next to me and kind of
perched on its back and made a speech as if he
were Moses or something. "We're actors!" He said
it like it had just occurred to him. "We need to be
going to auditions! Workshops! Agents!" His hair
was sticking up all over and his eyes looked kind
of wild. "This is our *new regime*—every morning
we'll hit the pavement and we won't quit until
sundown. We'll eat ramen noodles for supper,
because we'll have to be poor for a while. Then
we'll rehearse monologues with each other until
Letterman comes on. Then we'll have great sex.
. . ." At this point he jumped down and came over
to me—I was staring dumbly, as I recall—and
grabbed my pen and slammed it down in the
middle of the pickle recipes. He had me out of my
chair and out of my T-shirt in about one second,
and pretty soon we were crashing around the
kitchen like a couple of blind people dancing a

polka.

So of course I thought, Hello, Hollywood! Here comes Trudy Trommeter! I saw my face in one of those little squares on TV next to Meg Ryan and Sally Field and Michelle Pfeiffer and Meryl Streep, and Richard Gere's voice was saying "This year's Oscar for Best Actress goes to . . ." and then I heard the sound of the seal being broken and Richard's little gasp of surprise

We had a yard sale and sold the leftovers to Harry's Junque Shoppe on Lexington Avenue. I scrubbed and cleaned like a maniac so I could get my security deposit back. We put $500 down on a blue 1988 Astro, which was really in good shape when we got it, and we had exactly $332.84 left. I'm not that quick sometimes, but it didn't take a genius to figure out that $300 wasn't even enough to buy gas to L.A. When I pointed that out to Mel, he practically went apoplectic—slapping his knees, slapping his forehead, guffawing until tears came to his eyes. "L.A.!" he kept howling. And, "Gert, Gert, Gert," like he was just delighted with me and felt terribly sorry for me at the same time. When he finally calmed down, he cupped my face with his two strong hands, and looked right into my eyes with his blue ones, and said, like it was the wisest statement ever, "there are *two* coasts."

I felt my features sagging into their dumb look. I croaked, "I didn't think there was a significant demand for actors in Myrtle Beach." Mel seemed like he was going to start laughing again, but I guess my dumb look turned into an expression that made him change his mind.

"Of course we're not going to Myrtle Beach," he said patiently. "Wilmington—the new movie capital of the world!" He still had my face in his hands, and I felt like he was molding me into a Picasso as he spoke. "We'd get lost in L.A.—we'd just be two goldfish in the ocean. We can make it right here in North Carolina, and"—he finally let go and I tried to put everything back where it belonged—"no earthquakes!" I got the feeling we'd be eating ramen noodles for a very long time.

We hadn't even made it out of town when Carlos Arturo Valdez, who was about to miss his thirty-minute deadline on a Domino's pizza delivery, pulled out into the oncoming lane and bam! The Domino's insurance agent gave us a rental car that same night. It was a nice little Nissan, in a color the Avis girl called "greige." I felt greige. We drove it to Frank's Body Shop, where the van had been towed, and I suppose we would have been even more depressed if we had known how long it was going to take Frank to fix it, but we didn't know that then, and we were depressed as hell anyway. We got our main necessities of life and took a room at the Rockola Inn, which didn't have cable. We ordered pizza from the same Domino's where Carlos Arturo Valdez had worked and didn't tip the driver. Our ribs hurt.

The next afternoon we had $288.66 left, and Mel came up with a new plan: night jobs. The idea was, we would work the third shift and then sleep on the ground at some picnic area during the day, thus saving the cost of living at the Rockola. We figured we could slip into the Eleanor Roosevelt dorms for showers easily enough. I got a job at the 24-hour Wal-Mart, and while I worked Mel slept all scrunched up in the Nissan in the parking lot. I came out on my lunch break, usually to find the windows all fogged up and the radio still playing. That worried me—I kept thinking the battery would go dead. Usually I just ate and Mel slept, but once in a while he'd stir, and reach for me, and well, the windows being foggy and all. . . .

During the day, I slept outside. It really was kind of nice. Except when Mel would leave me at the bottom of some hiking trail on the parkway and go off. He was looking for a job, though, so I guess he had no choice. Once it rained really hard, and all I could do was huddle under a tree with my blanket wrapped around me. I was tired and cold and alone and I really hated Daniel Patrick Aquilino, a.k.a. Mel, at that particular point in time. The next day we got the tarp.

We kept going back to Frank's Body Shop for changes of clothes and to dump our dirty ones in the van. Frank kept saying he was waitin' on a part from Tennessee. Or that he was all backed up—Wayne got strep throat and Cecil was sittin' jury duty. He jist haddin got to it yet.

We got the van back on the same day the first payment was due. Frank took a picture of us next to it so he could hang it up on his bulletin board. (I saw it the next time we brought the van in. I'm wearing a real pretty smile—you'd never know I'd just written a check to Fairview Acceptance Corporation for $240.33 and we had exactly $54.78 left.)

Mel and I had our first real fight that night. Even though I was extremely p.o.'d and I kept calling him Danny, which he hates, somehow the sheer brutality of it made me feel we were closer than before. More like married. The next day he was hired by a mortuary company to sell mausoleum space door-to-door. Fairdinkum.

Mel is a born salesman. On my days off, I'd sometimes go with him. His main gimmick was the Australian accent. Women just loved hearing him talk. He'd be real cheerful about his "product," laughing at the expressions he'd get and reminding everyone that they were going to die. I think he had some of his customers actually looking forward to it before he left.

He'd worm his way into some sweet old lady's kitchen, and pretty soon she'd be bustling around to make him a cup of tea. Then he'd start reminiscing about "down home." He'd sing a line or two from *Rigoletto* and gaze off in memory for a moment. Then he'd turn his killer blue eyes on the poor old lady and calmly tell her how the construction crew uncovered an entire graveyard when they started digging at the Sydney Opera House site and a lot of the coffins were busted open, causing remains to be distributed helter-skelter. "There was no way to put those poor sods back together," Mel would say. I don't know about you, mum, but I'm for lyin' in a bed above ground,

where I won't be cause for a steam shovel opera-
tor to lose his lunch." He'd hold his grim look for
just the right beat, and then he'd burst into an
exuberant smile again. "Thought I would make a
good ghost for an opera house, right, mate?" He'd
start singing *Rigoletto* again and collecting his brochures, as though he was going to leave. The old
lady would beg him to sit down and have a refill
of his tea so they could talk business.

One perfectly ordinary morning, Mel pulled
out from a stop sign where he had only paused,
and a sixty-three-year-old schoolteacher who had
no patience for nonsense made mush out of the left
front quarter of the van. Mel didn't try to sell her
a mausoleum space.

This time there wasn't any Nissan. Mel talked
the Avis girl into giving us a white LeBaron convertible at the economy rate. The first place we
drove it to was Frank's. He looked sadly at the van
and said he'd git right to it.

The next day I got arrested. Mel had dropped
me off at Eleanor Roosevelt so I could clean up
while he made a call nearby. I took my usual lei-
surely shower, but I knew it would still be at least
an hour before he'd return. I was just sort of wan-
dering around in a daze when I found myself
outside Room 217, the room I had shared with Julie
Booth in my freshman year. Just looking at the
number on the door brought back the queerest
memory: the moths that congregated above the
cabinet where we kept our food. They were small
and dark and dusty, but they didn't bother us much

so we left them alone. Then one day, a few weeks after the moths just magically disappeared, we found a million little maggoty worms crawling on our ceiling. Julie was the squeamish type, but I got obsessed with the campaign against the moth larvae. The more I killed them, the more they came back. I was fighting a Chinese army of worms. Eventually I started smashing them bare-handed, smearing their guts all over the ceiling. It was no longer enough that they died; I wanted them to suffer. Julie told the R.A., and they bombed our room.

Standing outside 217 with my hair dripping, I was overwhelmed with curiosity. Would I find one little moth flitting innocently about? Would the entire ceiling be festering like an open sore? Would Julie be sitting on her bed, painting her toenails black? I turned the knob, and the door opened, and I felt like Alice must have when she walked through the looking glass.

The room smelled like lemons. There was a poster-size framed photo of a black girl in a riding habit holding the reins of a blacker horse. Her name was Tashonda Williams, and I found out later that she wasn't actually nine feet tall, but she seemed like it when she walked into her room and caught me trying to read the inscription on the gold pocket watch I'd picked up from her desk. She said, "What?!" and had me face down on her dhurrie bedspread with my arms pinned solid against my back in about three seconds.

They let me go on my own recognizance. I told

the magistrate I had taken a method acting assign-
ment a little too far. Tashonda dropped the charges
and gave me a ride back to Eleanor Roosevelt. In
the car, she told me the inscription on the watch
was "Remember me."

My panic attack felt like the opposite of panic.
I just shut down. I knew Mel was speaking to me,
but it was as if his volume was turned way low.
For the next few days I just sat and stared. I must
have gone to the bathroom, and I must have eaten
something. I guess I slept a lot. Mel took us back
to the Rockola Inn. You're probably going to think
that what he did there was bizarre, but all I can
say is I snapped out of it.

The first thing I remember is hearing Scottish
folk tunes. That was our local public radio's idea
of ethnic programming. Then I remember feeling
itchy all over. I tried to scratch my scalp, but I heard
Mel whisper, "Don't move." There was something
damp and heavy and sticky covering me. I blinked
hard to open my eyes. The ceiling was shimmering in candlelight. I smelled glue. Next thing I
knew the Scottish singers were drowned out by the
roar of my blow dryer. "You'll be done in a minute," Mel shouted.

Maybe I fell asleep again for a while, because
the next thing I remember is the weird sensation
that my skin was being lifted off. I sat up, naked
except for a film of oil and glue covering my body,
and saw Mel standing at my feet holding a life-size
reproduction of me, made out of newsprint. I want
to say, "I glanced around the room in bewilder-

ment," but bewilderment doesn't adequately describe the result of the glance. There were papier mâché me's everywhere. Only one full-size, which Mel was leaning against the wall, but lots of faces, torsos, bottom halfs, upper halfs, legs, arms—and they were painted and glittered and some had Easter grass hair, one was smoking a cigarette, and one had two marshmallows for eyes.

I didn't say anything. I just gave Mel this big question mark of a look and he came over and grabbed my gluey body as though he hadn't seen me in about ten years, and we kissed, and when I finally pulled away long enough to look at him I saw that he was crying and smiling. I don't know how we didn't end up glued together forever in the Rockola.

We snuck out of the motel room, leaving the effigy holding an "I'm sorry" sign and all the body parts scattered around in appropriate places: a hand on the fly swatter, legs sticking out from under the bed, etc. I thought the face staring up from the toilet bowl was going too far, but Mel almost got a hernia he laughed so hard.

We got to Frank's before he opened and stood with our hands gripping the chain-link fence, staring rapturously at the van. It was fixed. When Frank came and unlocked the big padlock on the gate, we were jumping up and down in excitement. Boy, what perfect timing, it looks brand-new, you sure are a pro, Frank. He took another picture of us, and Mel handed him the insurance check. That covered everything except the deductible, Frank said. Another two hundred fifty dollars and we could be on our way.

You've got to remember that Mel and I are trained actors. "Oops," Mel said, "left the checkbook in the car." I made small talk with Frank until Mel stuck his head through the door and yelled, "Gert!" His tone told me all I needed to know. I bolted, and before I even shut the door on the passenger side, we were peeling out.

Inside Daryl's E-Z Stop, I slipped and fell on purpose and pretended my ankle was broken so that Daryl and all the customers would be paying attention to me long enough for Mel to switch our tag with the one on the pickup truck that had a SHIT HAPPENS bumper sticker on the back. Then I miraculously recovered, and we got some egg salad sandwiches, six bottles of RC, a big bag of Doritos, a three-pack of Crackerjacks, two moon pies, and a cassette tape by Melissa Etheridge.

I guess we didn't make it onto the FBI's most wanted list, because there were no roadblocks or helicopters circling overhead as we slipped out of the county. Mel took backroads, and when it started to thunder and lightning and pour, we got lost. He pulled onto a dirt road, but it had become a mud road, and when we tried to turn around we slid into a Frazier fir, which took out the window of the panel door and left the door itself hanging by its upper track. Mel tied it to the frame of the seat with the drawstring cord from my sleeping bag, and he covered the gaping hole with the blue plastic tarp.

We spent our emergency ten-dollar bill in Chinquapin. Mel backed into a flatbed trailer and wrecked the whole rear end of the van in Duplin. Peytona is where we stopped, because we were about to run out of gas. We knew if the van got towed anywhere we'd have to execute another prison break, so we looked for the biggest parking lot in Peytona, which turned out to be the cannery at the edge of town. If the wind was blowing in the wrong direction, it was bad news for the people of Peytona. Boy, did that place stink—wet and warm, like fresh puke, only worse. That was probably why there was a JOB OPENINGS sign at the front entrance.

Mel and I were hired to sort corn. No experience necessary. All we had to do was stand in front of a conveyor belt and pick out the ears that looked bad. We were supposed to throw them in these bins that were strategically placed along the line, but I soon found out that the shots that actually made it into the garbage cans were the misses. The only job in the cannery more disgusting than ours was cleaning the floors, which were covered with rotten corn sludge.

Due to the unrelenting heat, we got a five minute break every hour to go outside and try to find some air to breathe. The other Peytona employees all looked like retired carnies. They averaged seven teeth per mouth. During our breaks, they stood around in small silent groups and smoked cigarettes, never wasting any inhaling time on conversation. But somehow, some of them found out that Mel and I were living in the parking lot, and when we trudged home after our third long day of sorting corn, we were surprised to find a cardboard carton of groceries next to the van. A note inside the box said, "From your friends at Peytona Cannery. Good luck and keep the faith." Without the food, we would never have made it to our first payday. Our combined earnings of $244 made us feel very flush then. The job was starting to seem not so bad, and that scared the shit out of us, so we left.

The first thing we did was fill the van with gas, which Mel said was enough to get us to the coast. Then we found a Wal-Mart and Mel got a pair of navy bermudas and three plain white Fruit-of-the-Loom T-shirts in a package, and I got white shorts and a white tank top because it was so hot, and one of those barrettes with a silky white bow attached, which would look really nice when I French-braided my hair, and we both got new underwear and deodorant and flip-flops. Then we got a room at a Motel 6 and argued all the way from the front desk to number 308 about who would get the shower first. When we turned the key and opened the door and the air conditioning hit us in the face, it was like diving into a pool. We raced each other to get naked, and discovered that even though a Motel 6 shower is pretty small, we could both fit in it and move around pretty well, too.

We found a little Italian restaurant called Nardo's, where we ate homemade minestrone, salad, and garlic bread, huge plates of mostaccioli, and washed it down with a bottle of valpolicella. There was one of those red fishbowl candles with netting stretched around it and Mel was staring at the flame, idly brushing garlic bread crumbs off the red and white plastic tablecloth, when he just came right out and said, "Trudy, will you marry me?" I don't know how my mouth suddenly felt so dry when there was still unswallowed wine in it, but it did. I put my glass down and just stared at him, but he was still looking down into the candle. His cheeks looked pink under his tan. I didn't say anything until he looked up. His blue eyes looked scared.

"Yeah, Danny," I whispered. I put my hand on his and we both smiled and laughed and I felt my eyes getting glisteny and saw that his were, too.

We sort of floated out of Nardo's and walked for a long time. Even at night it didn't cool off very much, but I felt perfect. When we saw the church, we both knew what we were going to do. It was a Catholic church, pretty big for a little southern town, and the door was open.

We walked through a vestibule that was made to look like the grotto at Lourdes with statuary of Bernadette kneeling before the Lady and dipped our fingers into the "miraculous pool," which was really a basin for holy water.

The church was empty. A few vigil lights flickered on the left side of the main altar. I could almost hear the music from *West Side Story* as Mel and I walked slowly down the center aisle, just like

Maria and Tony in the dress shop. We stood before the altar rail and Mel said, "I take you, Gertrude Mary Trommeter, to be my wife, until death." And I said, "I take you, Daniel Patrick Aquilino, to be my husband, until death." Mel pretended to lift a bridal veil from my face and we kissed. Then we walked hand in hand to the vigil lights, and we each lit a straw and together we lit a candle. Mel said do you love me? And I said I love you. He said do you trust me? And I said I trust you.

Then he took every bit of all the money we had in the world and stuffed it into the black box for vigil light donations. "We are the lilies of the field," he whispered.

I was raised Catholic, and I had never before spoken out loud in church except to pray or sing, but that night I screamed, "I divorce you!" three times at the top of my lungs and tore my brand-new white tank top. Mel chased me down the aisle shouting that I couldn't divorce him because we hadn't consummated the marriage yet, which I thought was extremely stupid since we'd been consummating our brains out for over two years. I got to the Motel 6 before him, but he had the key so I had to let him in. I told him if he even thought about getting in that bed with me I would cut off his penis.

The next day I still wouldn't speak to him, so we just rode along in silence, except for our stomachs, which were growling at each other. When the blub, blub, blub sound of a flat tire joined the sing-along I wasn't even surprised. I just gave Mel my most withering look. Then I got out and sat on the side of the road and watched him struggle to jack up the van, and that's when I started my period.

It's interesting that losing a contact made me see things more clearly. Or so I thought at the time. After I stopped crying, I just kept hearing my parents' voices, and I had this enormous revelation that they were right. Mel and I had been playing baby games all summer. We weren't like the people who really had to work at the Peytona cannery—if things got too rough, help was just a collect call away. I was tired of being a fake and I was tired of being hungry and I was tired of Mel. I was going to walk to the nearest pay phone and ask very politely for a bus ticket home.

When I told Mel what I had just discovered, his response was that adventures weren't always full of good luck and good times. He said you had to take risks and go out on limbs to catch your dreams. Everything sounded like a stupid cliché and I told him so. I said I was following the double yellow line to the nearest sign of civilization because there wasn't any Emerald City, pal, so have a great life. I was very irritated with myself for crying as I heard Mel shouting after me, "You should see yourself, Trudy! You're right in *the middle of the road!*" I shot him a bird.

I must have been walking for about an hour when I saw the dead possum. It wasn't all smashed and bloody—it was just lying there. I touched it. It was weird how it felt so real, because it looked light and empty. Like if you picked it up, it would just float in the air. Then I remembered how I had picked up my dog when he died, and he was so much heavier. *This could be me*, is what I thought. I knew, looking down at that possum, that I didn't give a damn what happened to me after I was dead, but I sure as hell cared about what happened between now and then. I wasn't exactly clear about everything I wanted, but I knew a whole bunch of things were never going to make it to the top of my list: a bed that won't hurt my back and a pen that won't run out of ink and pickle recipes from my mom were among them. And walking through life down the middle of the road.

I turned around. I don't know why I got all soupy over a dead possum, but my eyes were blurry, and that's why it took me a couple of minutes to realize that the small figure bobbing up and down on the horizon was Mel. In case you're getting ready to stick your finger down your throat, let me assure you that we did not run into each other's arms in slow motion like in a made-for-TV movie. Instead, the closer he got, the more I averted my eyes. I wasn't looking at him at all when we passed each other like two strangers out for a walk on the highway. I kept going, but my heart was pounding and my face was hot and my head felt all confused. *What the hell am I doing?* I kept asking myself. Then I felt Mel nearby, and I glanced over my shoulder.

"Quit following me," I said. I noticed he was out of breath, like he'd been running, and he was carrying both of our backpacks.

"You were right, Gert," Mel said. I couldn't believe how cheerful he sounded. It really pissed me off. "There isn't enough demand for actors on the East Coast. We've been heading the wrong direction. Let's not underestimate ourselves— we're good enough for the majors." His voice was shaking under his accent and his eyes had that scared look I'd seen before at Nardo's.

"Well," I said, and it came out real throaty, "if we could make it through this summer—how bad can California be?" Okay, now you can gag if you want to, because he dropped the backpacks and scooped me up and we kissed bigtime, and laughed and cried and hung on to each other for dear life.

A bunch of trucks passed us before one stopped, and we knew before we even got in that this one would be going all the way. As we settled back against the red vinyl upholstery, Langston— we found out later that was his name, and we called him "Langston our Savior," which he was— Langston started fiddling with the radio dial. He stopped just where the horns go, "doo-doo-doo-doo-doo" and the Beatles sing "All you need is love, love—love is all you need . . ." and they start shouting in the background and the music goes a little haywire and you hear, "she loves you, yeah, yeah, yeah . . . love is all you need, love is all you need, love is all you need . . ." Langston switched to something country, but that music stayed inside me.

A Way with Words

by Christopher Hawthorne

T he note is written in a neat, elegant hand. The printed script flows across four pieces of hotel stationery, which are crisp, like pages in a book opened for the first time.

Vivian Slocomb carries the note on flat, outstretched hands. She never realized until now what careful handwriting—beautiful in its preciseness— her son had, not until she could examine the note without actually reading it. She thinks now that he could have been a graphic artist. He had an eye for symmetry, and spacing, and color—always looking, seeing beauty in the oddest, out-of-the-way places, finding aesthetic pleasure where others found mere images or even distraction.

"I think you ought to read it," she says plainly. She has come upon her husband in the kitchen. He is leaning over the kitchen table, both hands gripping its edges, reading the newspaper. His hair is cut short—too short, she thinks, but it will grow out—and large reading glasses rest heavily on his nose.

"It's not written for us," he says, without looking up.

"Still, it's here. The words aren't going anywhere. It's been eight months, John."

"It's not a question of time."

"Well, what is it, then? Parts of it will make you smile."

"How many times have you read it?"

"Not enough to make up for you not reading it."

"It's not for us."

"What will it take?"

He says nothing. She waits a few seconds for a response, but his silence continues, his head down, his eyes staring blankly at the newspaper. She moves to a tall chair in the corner of the room and sits down carefully. She lifts the note close to her face, just below her chin.

The dishwasher emits a low hum. The neighbors on both sides are on vacation and the cat is asleep on the patio in the late afternoon sun and they are completely alone in the house. She begins to read.

10/13/69 - 8/03/92

The worst kind of poet is a dead one. He who writes his own eulogy—the man who seeks to give his words some kind of magical quality by attaching them to catastrophic fate, who thinks tragedy writes a breathtaking tale—is just as troublesome. What he fails to realize is that life is fullest in despair and death is a poor editor.

So I must preface these remarks with the warning that they are not intended as pop drama. It is just that I have never really written before, and though my fear of literary rejection outweighs my fear of death (apparently!), I had to give a voice to my experience. I have a song that runs in my head, a musical likeness that deserves verbal expression.

My words will precede me to wherever I am going and follow me from whence I came. They are my purgatory. Perhaps they will be my salvation—and yet, perhaps somehow they have hastened my demise. But I fear I am losing my audience; spiritual confusion, after all, does not a gripping story make. So allow me to describe the events about which I am certain.

I killed myself on August 3, 1992, in Oakland, California, by sticking a .38 revolver in my mouth and firing one shot. It was a dreary day—the fog never lifted, as it usually does around noon during the summer.

The gun was colder than I expected, its steel like smooth rock hidden in the shady recesses of a quarry, cooled by its own darkness. It was rude. I tried to get to know it; I held it close against my cheek and between my fingers; it refused even to tell me its name. I would have liked to call it she in these pages, but the gun turned out to be a thing, plain and simple. A straightforward, rather elegant machine. Cold ebony death rushing past my face even as I gripped it and sang to it.

I was stoned the day I did it. I had been smoking weed a lot in the last few weeks. It was my only remaining hobby. I never could even smoke a cigarette without coughing violently, but the yellow smoke of pot rushed down my throat with a pleasant urgency. What I like about weed is the same thing I like about good writing. It makes the rational irrational and the irrational beautiful.

The only writing I did before this was some poetry I put together while I was baked. Its jumpy syntax somehow struck me as rhythmic.

> Peopled islands are in my nightmares
> The object of desire is obscured.
> Resuscitation resides
> In a gray cloud that
> Dissipates when struck by the
> Sun of ambition—
> Singly motivated, enviable.

—or—

> A vignette is silly when you are in it.

I liked those but knew they weren't quite right—meaning, of course, that they weren't quite wrong. *I agonized for weeks about whether to change "obscured"* to "obscure." Then as I was walking downtown one day I came up behind a tourist who was wearing one of those ridiculous attempts at Japanese coolness, The Shirt with Random English Words on It. I had seen a similar one while in line at Disneyland, but this one was better. In tall, stitched letters that appeared to be losing their cohesion as the shirt stretched, I read the poem I had been trying for so long to write:

> For Yankee girl
> Daisy and Milky
> MASS HYSTERIA
> Boy and Girl
> All ticket sold out

It was sublime, and I was devastated. Yet I walked back to my car with a renewed sense of purpose, in one of those moods brought on by the discovery of genius. It was then I knew I had to kill myself.

I considered several options. Immediately sleeping pills were out—they're always associated with the attempted suicide, never the successful one. People magazine is full of stories about the depressed former child star who, we are told in hushed tones, swallowed a whole bottle of sleeping pills, only to wake up in a chi-chi clinic in Van Nuys, wondering what happened, a sweating bottle of Evian waiting on the bedside table. And besides, I didn't want to sleep. I wanted to die.

I considered the carbon monoxide bit, running a tube from the exhaust pipe inside the car, the closed garage and all that, but I didn't have a car. Jumping from a bridge, or a tall building, was of course attractive, but I rejected that because of the chances it might draw publicity to my death. I preferred a quiet end.

I settled on shooting myself. Not too expensive, uncomplicated, didn't require a degree in physics (mine was in French Literature). But I had to be careful. If I was going to shoot myself, I was going to do it right. The first time. No second attempts for me, no way I was going to let the gun slip and end up deformed but alive. Fuck that. Remember that kid who made a suicide pact with his friend, allegedly spurred on by Judas Priest lyrics? They went to a schoolyard at dusk. He watched his friend shoot himself and then when he picked up the shotgun he was shaking so hard he blew his face off instead of brains out. And then he had to testify at the trial—his parents versus the band—looking like some kind of traveling freak show. His face had slid right off his skull like cheese off a hot pizza.

I was not going out like that. One shot, straight through the brain, plain and simple. A little messy for whomever had to clean me up, but from my end a streamlined process.

I bought the gun in West Oakland, in a shop on San Pablo Avenue that was covered on the outside by fake wood paneling. The guy who sold it to me was a fat man with a beard and suspenders and a tattoo of Abe Lincoln on his right forearm. I felt a slight twinge when I realized I could get the gun right away, that day. Two years earlier, home from Princeton for the summer, I had canvassed door-to-door in Marin County for the Brady Bill, which called for a mandatory waiting period for the purchase of firearms.

I bought the gun and four bullets for $193. The

*fat man with suspenders and the tattoo wrapped it up
and put it into a large green bag. I walked out of the
gun shop and into the sharp early-evening sunlight. My
shadow was elongated by the setting sun, and as I
neared my car it bounced against the squat buildings.
I held up my arm and in the shadow it reached the
second floor.*

*I turned the corner toward my car, passing under
a freeway on-ramp. To my right, I noticed a mural
painted in taut, bright colors, and somehow I saw myself
in the middle of its spinning rays, saw my thin limbs
and flimsy dreams, and saw the green bag and the gun
and my death. It was a stunning scene, almost pastoral
in its integrity.*

*I drove home, to the house where I lived with my
parents. Since graduating from Princeton I had been
working in Berkeley, selling futons on commission. I
made about $300 a week. I was saving money to go to
Tibet. Our house was high in the Oakland hills, with a
shining view of the Bay Area sprawled out beneath
almost every window. The vista always appeared blue-
gray to me, even on the brightest of days, for the sun
around here has a way of drawing all the color from the
objects it strikes below. Rather than energize them, it
seems instead to give them the look of a gaunt child.
(Not that a gaunt child cannot be beautiful, I should
add, for I did love the view. It had a limited palette, that
was all.)*

*I didn't hide the gun. I stuck it on the bedside table,
still in the bag, under the stack of books there. I was
reading a lot of Nietzsche in the weeks before I died.*
When virtue has slept, she will get up more re-

freshed. *I know—quoting Nietzsche out of context is about as responsible as, well, about as responsible as sticking a loaded .38 in your mouth and pulling the trigger. Sometimes I would read Nietzsche as fast as I could, my eyes rushing over the words, trying to feel the pace of his intent.* How did reason come into the world? As is fitting, in an irrational manner, by accident. One will have to guess at it as at a riddle.

The gun ticked in the night. I lay in bed beside it and felt somehow comforted by its presence. Sometimes I would take the gun out of the bag and hold it in front of my face, just barely able to make out its outline in the darkness. I liked to snap out the chamber and spin it, just like they do in the movies, spin it and hold it up to my ear and listen. Then I'd put it away in the bag and put the bag on the bedside table under the books and wake up in the morning refreshed and ready for the day ahead.

I felt an odd contentedness at work those last few weeks. My sales went way up. I became so animated during my speech to customers that I would often lie down on the futons myself, or invite the customers to do so, two things I normally never did. (Too showy.) I treated my sales pitch on the difference between the six- and eight-inch foam mattress as if it were great oratory. This is your trade, I told myself. Practice it faithfully.

I even gave my boss two weeks' notice. He asked why I was quitting and I told him to travel to Asia. Tibet? he asked. Tibet, I said. I made a joke about wanting to become a sherpa. He laughed slowly.

On August 3, around 2:30, I checked into the Red Lion Hotel at the Oakland Airport. My room was large.

It had two double beds, a bedside table, and another small table with two chairs, where I wrote this. The room was decorated in red and orange and the cups in the bathroom were wrapped in clear plastic. The window looked out on the back parking lot.

I sat on the bed nearest the door and read USA Today *and watched television. They had one of those remote controls that is bolted to the bedside table and swivels. It was kind of a drag, because I was restless, switching channels a lot, and my back began to get sore.*

I stuck the green bag with the gun in it in the second drawer of the bedside table, under the thick Bible. I had my Nietzsche book with me, too, and I tossed that on the floor in front of the television. I packed a bowl in my pipe and set it on top of the alarm clock. They had a "Studs" marathon on; I watched three shows in a row and then, at 4:30 in the afternoon, I watched SportsCenter on ESPN and lit the pipe and smoked the whole bowl. The room spun and I watched the end of Bonnie and Clyde. *Suddenly I had shifting planes of beige regret moving inside my body but soon I was OK. I wanted to smoke another bowl but I had writing to do.*

At about 6:00 I ordered a room service dinner: fried chicken and a Beck's and a small green salad. The total came to $11.37 and I gave the guy who brought it a $5 tip. I told him not to pick up the dishes until the next day. He was the last person I ever saw. After I ate I sat down at the table and wrote this note.

At 8:15, I drew the bolt on the door and closed the drapes and sat down on the edge of the second bed. It was cleaner, neater, than the bed I had been sitting on, and I appreciated its expanse of unruffled covers. I pulled out the green bag and reached in without looking. I gripped the gun and then withdrew it and placed it on the bed beside me. I pulled out the box of bullets and loaded the chamber.

I reached back and, twisting my back again, hit the mute button for the television. There was also a remote panel that controlled the lights so I turned them all off with one finger. The flashing screen of the television stood out now, so that if I had opened the drapes someone standing in the parking lot would have noticed blue light flickering against the walls of the room.

I cocked the gun. I stroked it absently, holding it against my leg as I stared at the silent images on television. I too have been in the underworld, like Odysseus, and I shall yet return there often; and not only sheep I have sacrificed to be able to talk to a few of the dead, but I have not spared my own blood. *"Headline News" was on. As soon as a commercial came on I placed the gun in my mouth. As soon as the anchorwoman returned to the screen I pulled the trigger.*

To the reader: I wrote this note between 7:00 and 8:15 p.m. on August 3, 1992. As I was still alive when I wrote it, the passages concerning events after 8:15 that evening are projected. But I assure you they occurred just as I have related them to you. It was all carefully planned, you understand.

The tenses here may cause you some trouble. For this I apologize. I think the way I have arranged things relates the drama of the event best.

*I have written all of this down so that it may stand
in the semi-public record, in case I do something to
become famous one day. (Fame is powerful like that—
she can rearrange events as she pleases.) I want to give
people something with which to see into my psyche a
little bit.*

For I know I will be great.

She looks up slowly, and finds that her
husband's head is still lowered. It appears immov-
able. But soon he turns, and she notices that his
face looks less tired than she expected it would.

"Damn it, I always said he could write, didn't
I?" he asks quickly, and she agrees with a silent
nod. Readjusting his glasses, he continues. "If I
didn't know it was him, I might have been enter-
tained by that. But I suppose that was the point."

They walk out the front door together and sit
down in the thick grass, and in the waning light
they begin to contemplate the front garden.

This fictional story is dedicated to the memory of
Ryan Taylor. It was completed before his death.

The Mary Pictures

by Kathy Conner

The Mary Pictures, souvenirs of a summer I'd all but forgotten, artifacts of a girl who didn't behave. I can't believe they survived, but here they are, living testimony to the fact that no matter how old I get or how hard I try, there is no figuring out my mother. As good as buried for almost twenty years, the pictures resurfaced when we were getting ready for the big yard sale that would pave the way for Momma's move to Florida.

Momma had finally decided to give up the

house and move in with Aunt Gladys. Seeing as how they were both lonely and long distance calls were eating up their savings, it seemed the natural thing to do. I'd only suggested it about a million times in the years since Daddy had died, but Momma always said no, that she was hanging on to the house for her grandchildren's sake. That's Momma for you, a martyr from the word go. She has no grandchildren because I've let her down.

My divorce hit Momma harder than it hit me or Jeff. For us, it came as a relief, kind of like when you know it's gonna break your heart to put the dog to sleep, but a little voice is whispering in your head, "Won't it be sort of nice not to be vacuuming up all them dog hairs all the time?" Come to think of it, Jeff was a lot like Skippy, cute and lovable, but in the long run more trouble than he was worth. He needed to run, if you know what I mean.

Anyhow, Momma took our breakup as the next to last nail in her coffin. She took the money she'd put aside for the grandkids' education and went to Orlando to see Gladys and Mickey Mouse. Next thing you know, she was back, marveling about a shuttle bus that ran every three hours from Gladys's condo to the mall and back. Now, I'd been providing Momma with that kind of service for the past three years, but to hear her talk, you'd think she'd seen it invented before her eyes at Ocean Shores. She and Gladys decided then and there to hook up and pool their resources, both wondering why it hadn't occurred to them before.

We didn't even have to advertise the house,

just called up the slick realtor who'd been coming by regularly since the zoning had gone commercial. A developer was putting in a mess of storage shelters across the road and wanted to operate out of our house. After the project was done, a caretaker for the storage town would move in. Progress. Momma just wanted to know where to sign—that's how eager she was to get to work on the yard sale.

In Beckley, West Virginia, a yard sale is a major social event: trotting out your old Pyrex measuring Cups and Tupperware without lids as if they were debutantes over in Charleston. Momma was in her glory, making an inventory of things she'd held on to for a lifetime and was now willing to set out on a card table with a piece of posterboard that said: "All items on this table under $2" and a big yellow smiley face.

I gritted my teeth and called her up. "Momma, what can I do to help?"

"Well, I'm going to ask you to do the same thing I've been asking since you were five years old—namely, clean up your room. You go through there and see what you want or don't want. It's now or never, 'cause what I don't sell at the yard sale is going next day to the Goodwill."

Now, I could've been truthful and told her, "Momma, there's not a thing in my old room worth what it would cost to haul it over here," but that would've opened me up to hearing the family tree of every stick of furniture and every knickknack in the house. Why, didn't I remember the day that she and Daddy had gone down to the Lumberteria and bought the cinderblocks and boards to make me bookshelves 'cause I had gotten such a good report card that said I was in the top reading group? She had personally painted the boards blue in honor of the group's namesake, the bluebird. And what had I done? In my excitement, I had put the books on the shelves before the paint had dried and Daddy'd had to pay a big library fine when he returned all the storybooks trimmed in bluebird blue.

Sure I remember it, Momma, who wouldn't? But Momma forgets what she wants to forget or needs to forget. She could go on Oprah for a show on selective amnesia. I wouldn't dare remind her that the bookshelf story ends with me getting whipped for making the mistake, whipped with a switch she made me hunt down and cut for myself. No, it was easier to just go over with a U-Haul, pick up my childhood debris and cart it back to my place.

When I got there, Momma was out back in the shed with Reverend Paul, giving him first crack at the yard equipment. The church had a big riding mower, but he was interested in Daddy's old rotary push-mower for going in between the graves in the little cemetery behind the church. Momma's been weeding and mowing it voluntarily since she'd buried Daddy, and she wanted to leave her tools behind to give her peace of mind on that score.

"Hey, Reverend Paul, how ya doing?" I smiled

at our old friend.

"Well, Katie bar the door, you look like a teenager in those dungarees. How you doing yourself?"

He'd been saying "Katie bar the door" to me since I was five years old and singing in the cherub choir. His daughter Marsha was my best friend in those days. He was like family.

"I'm going to have to excuse myself," I told him. "Buddy's letting me have the U-Haul for free so I don't want to tie it up too long in case he gets a paying customer. He's offered to come over and help me load up the heavy stuff once I get it all sorted out."

"Sure, you go on along. Your momma's writing down my marching orders so I know who gets the real flowers and who gets the plastic. Last time I did the mowing, I moved all the doodads so I could maneuver the mower and everyone's decorations got mixed up. Mrs. Hunt liked to have died herself when she saw Grover's grave decked out in artificial." Reverend Paul's told that story a hundred times if he's told it once, but his dimples and twinkling eyes make me happy to hear it everytime.

Except for the bookshelves, my old room was pink, pink, pink, and ruffled, Momma's idea of what a little girl should covet in terms of interior decorating. She spent weeks making up the dotted swiss curtains, first enrolling herself in the "Sewing for the Home" class over at Adult Ed where she learned to call curtains "window treatments." If Momma could've found a way to wear those window treatments to Easter service, she would have, that's how proud she was. And she got me a rose colored shag rug, so shaggy I joke about learning my trade on it. Before they got the air conditioning put in, I passed many a hot, sleepless summer night on the cool wood floor, making pink braids in the throw rug. To this day, I can be French braiding a client and, for a second, feel my fingers in the pink wool. Some clients more than others, of course.

That morning, awash in pink, I settled myself in the middle of my old twin bed and, one at a time, emptied the dresser drawers, making three piles: keep, give away, toss. Toss was a big old pile of notebooks, headbands, and mangy stuffed animals. But keep turned out to be a bigger heap than I would have dreamed. There was my Betsy McCall doll with her nurse outfit from *McCall's* magazine and her pink dotted swiss formal, which Momma and I had fashioned from curtain scraps. There was every report card from my educational career, starting with Miss Gingrich's first grade right up through Roosevelt High, the early grade school ones saying without fail, "Katie is a fine student, but is inclined to excessive chatting with her classmates," or some variation on that theme. I ended the fine student half of the equation when I hit Roosevelt and devoted my entire time and attention to the chatting with classmates half. Boy classmates especially, which accounts for a lot of old letters and corsages in the keep pile. I was in the

Sweetheart Court three years straight and Christmas Queen my senior year and Daddy'd photo-
graphed me every step of the way, from putting
on my makeup to getting into the car with my date.
Momma had saved them all, neatly labeling the
backs. "Katie and Chuckie Slawson on way to
Sweetheart Dance, Feb. '71." The keep pile got so
big, I had to go into Momma's stash of moving
boxes which she'd been steadily collecting on her
trips to the Food Lion.

When I opened the bottom dresser drawer, I
smiled the unexpected smile of one meeting up
with an old friend. The Mary Pictures. I'd forgotten all about them, but there they were, stacked flat,
a little crinkly and cracked, but so familiar that for
a little while, I was once more Katie at Bible Camp
in the Arts and Crafts Pavilion.

I went to Vacation Bible School, deep in
Virginia's Shenandoah Mountains, every summer
between fourth and ninth grade, and after that
returned twice as a junior counselor. The whole
First Lutheran Sunday School went on the church
bus, Reverend Paul leading us in song: "Oh the B-
I-B-L-E, yes that's the book for me, I stand alone
on the word of God, the B-I-B-L-E!" That was leaving Beckley. An hour into the trip, the boys usually got around to striking up a resounding rendition of "The worms crawl in, the worms crawl out,
the worms play pinochle on your snout." You've
got to hand it to Reverend Paul for being a good
sport.

The Arts and Crafts Counselor was always an

art major from a Lutheran college somewhere, like Nancy Mullen from Thiel College in Pennsylvania. I met Nancy right around the heyday of Nancy Sinatra, who Momma called a "bona fide died-in-the-wool tramp." I loved Nancy Sinatra, and somehow I kept imagining that Nancy Mullen might also sing "These Boots Are Made For Walkin." I liked the part at the end that went, "Are you ready, boots? Start walkin'!" Still do. Momma's taste in music ran more toward Tennessee Ernie Ford singing gospel and "I owe my soul to the company store."

Nancy Mullen caught my fancy because she was obviously, even to my innocent eyes, flat out in love with the lifeguard down at the lake. I studied Nancy that summer as if there was going to be a final exam on seduction at summer's end. Under her guiding hand we specialized in landscapes—actually lakescapes—carting the art supplies and easels down the mountain path to the spot where Nancy would turn to us with a smile, tucking her hair behind her ears, and say, "Now you all draw nature and try to focus on shadows and light." Sure, Nancy. Us sixth-grade girls focused on Nancy untucking her blouse, tying it under her breasts, and Nancy hanging on the lifeguard stand, fiddling with her hair.

Then the day came when Reverend Paul and the camp director wandered down the mountain path to the lake to find Nancy and the lifeguard liplocked, Bible campers gazing on from a respectful distance. Reverend Paul was a good sport, but he had his limits. The lifeguard was sent packing and Nancy and her protégées were henceforth and forevermore restricted to indoor arts and crafts in the dining hall, which they called the arts and crafts pavilion during non-meal times. A less exciting and now tucked in Nancy told us to paint our favorite scenes from the Bible—God's Greatest Hits, so to speak.

I contemplated Eve, confident that apples and serpents lay well within my artistic range, but then the age-old problem of covering her nakedness reared its ugly old head. I knew that fig-leaf or no, I'd be in for a mess of teasing from the worms in the snout contingent. So I turned in my time of need to an old friend, Mary, mother of Jesus, whom I had portrayed not too long ago in the Pageant of Peace, having risen through the ranks of the heavenly host of angels and shepherds tending their flocks by night. Not to mention my kindergarten debut as a sheep in the aforementioned flock.

I painted the Virgin Mary in tempera for five days straight, yielding three portraits of the holy mother. And in each rendering, Mary looked more and more like Nancy Mullens. All she lacked was a Thiel College sweatshirt.

There was Mary being turned away from the inn with big tears flowing from eyes heavily lined in black with lids shadowed blue and spikey mascara lashes. The inn was a Holiday Inn in honor of Christmas. And there was Mary visited by the archangel, hearing the results of her pregnancy test and looking mightily surprised, captured for posterity with her passion pink manicure covering her gaping mouth. And finally, there was Mary, ascended into heaven, looking radiant in her new frosted blond shag cut, her pierced ears sporting peace symbol earrings.

I loved my Mary pictures and so did my girlfriends, who treated me with new respect on account of my artistic ability. Reverend Paul, seeing my work, burst out with a big belly laugh and, wrapping his arm around my shoulder to protect my feelings, said, "Hail Mary, full of grace, wash the makeup off your face!" He went on over to the first-aid station, which was also the kitchen, and got the nurse who was also the cook to come look, and even though they laughed, it was a smiling laugh and I basked in the spotlight.

At the end of our two weeks at camp, we gathered up our sleeping bags and shower sandals and unopened boxes of writing-home stationery and boarded the bus. Reverend Paul and the other grownups packed up our arts and crafts projects for the annual art show that took place in the church Fellowship Hall the first Sunday after camp. Momma was on the Hospitality Committee, so she was busy making punch out of green sherbet and ginger ale when the show was getting set up. By the time she saw the Mary pictures, it was too late. Half the congregation had already viewed my artwork and Momma had already been "disgraced beyond repair." She gripped my wrist tight as a tick on a dog and marched me out to the car, saying under her breath over and over, "How could you? How could you? I've never been so ashamed." And poor Daddy. Back home, he suggested she might be overreacting and that was all it took to send her to the bedroom, slamming the door behind her, leaving Daddy to worry about Sunday supper, which ended up being grilled cheese, the only cooking he knew how to do. To this day, the buttery aroma of grilled cheese in the frying pan calls up a picture in my mind of Daddy.

In view of Momma's hysterics on the day of the art show, I fully expected that the Mary pictures had been long ago burned up in the wood stove if they had made it past the dumpster in the church parking lot. Their resurrection tapped into a heretofore undiscovered vein of tenderness toward Momma. Who was this woman, bless her heart, who would painstakingly preserve these souvenirs of her day of infamy? I gently sandwiched the Marys between two heavy pieces of cardboard and carried them out to the U-Haul and laid them on the front seat. Momma and Reverend Paul were sitting in the kitchen sipping iced tea made elegant with mint leaves from her garden. My heart was too full to trust myself to speak right then, but I had already decided on a sentimental way to thank Momma for the Marys.

Momma had always admired *The Last Supper* painting and had it on a china plate propped up on display on the dining room hutch. I would atone for the Marys by painting a close-up of Jesus at the Last Supper, copied straight off her plate, no embellishments, no makeovers. I got out a stack of newspapers and started boxing up all of Momma's best dishes and figurines, labeling them "Florida/Dining Room," hoping that Gladys would have room to accommodate it all. The Last Supper plate I slipped into my tote bag and carried home. It sat on top of my stereo for a full month or more before I got around to doing something with it, being busy with the move and all. But once Momma was safely in Florida, bickering with Gladys, I went down to the Art Stop and shopped for paints, brushes, and canvas board. I worked for three weeks on capturing Jesus, surprised at how my professional expertise kicked in when artistic flair failed. Jesus's skin was flawless with olive undertones. His hair was a honey brown with strands of silver blond woven throughout. It helped a lot that I had a client, Lacey Bridges, with exactly that hair and I had perfected the ash blond streaks over the years of doing her. Jesus's robes gave me the most trouble, but I did the best I could and finally, I signed *Katie* on the bottom right-hand corner. I gave the painting an extra week to dry, having long since learned my lesson about rushing up the drying process, and then I packed it up to send to Florida along with a check to cover the cost of framing so they could match it up with their dinette set. Driving home from the post office, I felt like I had come full circle, that Momma and I were about to embark on a closer, albeit long distance, relationship. I fully expected her to call me up on receipt of the painting, but instead she sent me a letter.

Dear Katie,

Whew! It is hotter than you-know-what down here, so me and Gladys are staying put in the air conditioning. We hung up your painting of Willie Nelson over the t.v. I never much cared for him on account of all those wives, each one younger than the last, but Gladys has his album of hymns which includes "The Garden" (He walks with me and He talks with me), and I must confess I am seeing him in a new light. I had forgotten all about your gift for Art which you get from your father. I can't draw a straight line to save my soul. Speaking of your father, don't forget to go by the church and make sure someone is tending the cemetery. Well, it's time for our program. Gladys says tell you hi and that she likes the picture too. There is no one down here who can cut hair like you, I look like the wrath of God. I wish you were closer.

God Bless,
Momma

War Hero

by Bill Cotter

There's a big vacant lot a few streets down off Pumpkin Street that crowds up with weeds in the summertime as tall as me, and that's where the war is. The other kids let me start playing when I was about five, but they've been playing war there for years and years every summer night till it gets too dark to see. Back then we'd split up a bunch of neighborhood kids into two sides, and one side would try to take over the other side by taking prisoners or stitching somebody, which means to take them out of the war by hitting them with a dirt clod or a firecracker or something depending on the rules. We always followed the rules, at least back then we did.

I used to take a lot of pain and hits, probably because I was an easy target, a girl and littler than just about everybody. Sometimes I was a decoy or a kamikaze, and sometimes I had to steal the hose from the Macks' yard across the fence and make mudballs sitting in a ditch all day. That was mainly to keep from getting caught.

The best strategy was always to get a prisoner, because stitching somebody is harder than it sounds, you had to get a solid hit and we'd always argue about it too much. If you capture a prisoner, you'd have to bring them back down over to your base and get them to defect to your side by making them say "Give." You could twist their arm or do some other little torture to get then to give, and if they did, then they were on your side for the rest of the war, and that could last for a week sometimes. We had one war a couple of summers ago that lasted twenty days until Stew Vokes caught Pauline and we could all hear her shriek a word that sounded like *give* all across the lot at dusk on the last day, making the fireflies start up all at once. She never said what the torture was that he did.

I used to give easy, but I got tougher and it started into a little game with the other kids to get me to give. Sometimes the whole war would be just about me. My side would protect me or try to anyway, and the other side put all their time and direction into catching me and getting me to give.

The last couple of summers we haven't divided up into teams, we just keep more or less the same kids on the same sides and we're all pretty much solid lifetime enemies on and off the vacant lot. We get into fights at school and at the parking lot at the 7-Eleven or wherever, and there's a lot of ambushes, too. Once Colette got her leg broken when Ben Carvalho hit her blindside on his minibike, thinking she was Amanda. Colette and Amanda are sisters and they've always hated each other, always found each other on opposite sides of everything, including every war I can remember. Colette's always on our side, along with Alan, Ben, Pauline, Shine, Freddy, and Derek. The other side's usually Stew, Manny, John C., John M., Amanda, Scott, Julie, and Valerie. In order to even up if somebody doesn't show, we usually drop Freddy or Pauline, and they drop Val or Little John Mars, cause they're all littler and weaker. They used to drop me. You can't play if you're older than sixteen.

The time it was real war was last summer. Something changed then; maybe it was just the heat. It was much hotter than usual, every day the asphalt would melt and the straight roads would disappear into wavy heat lines, and you squinted all day and never got used to the sun. Everybody's hair lightened into blond, streaked with dirt; even Shine's black hair crinkled into kind of a dust color. Probably was dust.

It was a day like that when me and Pauline were hanging around the 7-Eleven on Campbell and Stew and Julie came across on bikes and stopped by the pay phone. Julie leaned up against the phone booth and looked at us and didn't blink or move when Stew slapped her on the butt, sneered at us, and went into the store. She lit a cigarette and shifted her hips to play with a pedal on her bike. She was wearing a man's white shirt tied in a halter and cutoffs with an apple core patch on the crotch. Her dark eyes stared straight at Pauline and me as she rocked slowly on the bike, clicking the pedals backwards every couple seconds, probably in rhythm to a song in her head. Her neck was wet with sweat and there was a wet crease at her waist where she stuck her hip out to the side to rest her hand with the cigarette. She's a year older than me and everybody knows that Stew and her go to bed together. Stew took pictures of her with no clothes on that I saw once. There's an old, broken gray prison bus outside of town near the silo by the tracks where kids go to smoke and drink, and I recognized the gray plastic bus seats she was stretched across in those Polaroids. She looks like she's eighteen and doesn't care what people know, and as hot as it was that day she looked as cold as dry ice by that phone booth staring at us sitting against that shady 7-Eleven wall. Pauline picked a tiny sliver of glass out of her bare foot. "You think they do it?"

" 'Course." Probably every day. "Why?"

"I don't know." Pauline scratched at the pavement with a straw.

"Forget it. You're too young." Pauline was eleven. She looked up at Julie, still rocking to that song. "She'd kill you anyway. Look at her."

Pauline didn't look. She scratched at the pavement again and threw the straw at a dumpster. A cop car went by with sirens on and faded out of town toward the refinery. Julie's dad nearly killed another guy in a fight after a nightshift at the refinery a few years ago, after the guy said something about the pictures that Stew took. Her dad had just gotten out of jail. I saw him driving around in an old brown Chevy with a padlock and a bent coathanger holding the trunk down.

"No, she won't," Pauline said as Stew came out and Julie stopped rocking. She kept staring at us as he gave her a pack of Marlboros and a Dr. Pepper, then flicked her cigarette at us hard, but it landed near my foot and glowed in the shade of the 7-Eleven. They rode off standing on the pedals and slanting through traffic on Campbell, then they were gone down an alley. We sat for a while while I smoked Julie's cigarette. It had greasy pink lipstick on it.

"What's that mean, huh?" I asked Pauline, who pulled up her knees a little.

"Nothin'," she said. "Let's go."

That afternoon war started on time, but I got caught quick by Stew. In the middle of the lot near the left side is a big pile of dirt and chunks of concrete and he grabbed me there and put me in a hammer-lock on the ground after I tripped on

some fishline he'd put down, and he pulled me off
to his camp in the back right corner of the fence
by the tire place. We were alone. He tied my foot
to the fence with some yellow plastic rope. Last
time he caught me I wouldn't give and I got to go
back to my camp, no hassle. This time he twisted
up a corner of his mouth and looked down at me
lying in the dirt and spit hard and disgusting on
my leg. He pulled a big old Buck knife out of his
back pocket and opened it with a greasy click
against his fingers.

"Give," he said.

"You're a fucker, Stew." He stepped on my
arm and put the point of that knife on my cheek
and I looked up and saw a different person almost.
One time I went down to Lake Delilah by myself
and there was Stew, and I saw him drown a yel-
low-striped cat with some string and a crowbar. He
was all by himself and he looked then like he did
standing over me, like he had no more on his mind
than taking out the trash.

Very quiet, "Give."

No. He nicked my cheek a little with the knife
and I whimpered. He let his foot up off my elbow
and slapped the back of my head with his knuckles. He's three years older and bigger than me and
I was afraid he was just going to sit right on me,
but he settled back and sat down behind me where
I couldn't see him. I kept my face in the dirt. He
was quiet, and me too, and soon I could hear the
other kids creeping around the lot and the traffic
on Carnation and the whistle of locusts and feel-

ing like I almost might fall asleep when he was suddenly kneeling on the backs of my thighs and leaning his hand on the back of my neck with one finger nearly in my ear and I felt that hot edge under my shirt and he slit it right up the back and I squeezed out "Give!" through the gap in my teeth and started crying, but he didn't let up until he'd cut my shirt off me and pitched it out in the weeds, where it hung between two thistles like a spider web. "You give, Mattie," he said to my temple in a voice with sand around it, "you always give."

Stew's side won the war that day. He stayed close to me and gave me his shirt to wear, didn't say anything, just took it off. He put his arm around me a couple of times. I've been afraid of him since, until now.

My brother George died from drowning a long time ago. He was a lot older than me. Mom keeps all his old stuff out in the garage in long cardboard boxes that I used to hunt through to get stuff for war, but there wasn't much of any use there except for a Daisy BB gun he used to shoot at paper targets in the alley behind the house. He picked off a bird one day that landed on the car and Mom took the gun away.

About a week after Stew cut off my shirt, on a day that was even stiller and hotter, I shot him with that gun. The weeds were paper-colored and crackly and there were no clouds in the sky and everybody was being cruel and playing just barely by the rules, and I was lying stomach down over by the back of the fence where the weeds were thicker when I saw him climb over the dirt hill and turn around and look at the fence. I squeezed one off and Stew screamed and I found out when I ran over to check him out like I didn't know what happened that I'd hit him in the eye. No one thought I did it or even knew exactly what happened, except for Pauline, who swore she wouldn't say anything. I went back to the lot after midnight to sneak the gun back home and put it back in the box in the garage. The next day it came out that Stew was shot and he'd most probably be blind in that eye. He is. Stew didn't play war again that summer and most of the other kids around just played a half-ass game, because Stew was the one who got the game rolling, they all said. A month later the whole lot burned up after Big John Coombs tried to launch about fifty bottle rockets at our camp through the weeds. Nobody got busted for that, but we didn't play again that summer and it was that school year we found out about the gun.

This isn't the BB gun I used that I'm talking about. There was a lot of talk around school about Stew having a real gun and he was gonna kill whoever blinded him and he knew who it was now. I didn't believe he knew it was me; there were plenty other kids who hated his guts, too. I wasn't anything special that way, and there were tons of kids there at the lot that day. Some kids were saying he had a 30.06 and other people said it was a big Magnum and Freddy Muskie said it was a fat sawed-off shotgun and he'd seen it and it was oily and heavy as a big can of paint. I wasn't worried about all this until Pauline started acting weird around me, not coming over when she said she would and talking to me like I was a little kid who was bugging her all the time. She told me once that I was like a roomful of gnats around her. I found out later after I hadn't seen her for a while that she was hanging heavy with Stew all of a sudden and all the kids around were saying that they were going to bed together and that Stew dumped Julie because he'd scored Pauline as a kid and Julie was spent. That was a couple of months ago.

Later I saw Julie for the last time. She came up to me while I was punching for a Coke outside the ValueMaxx, and she said, "Hey."

"Hey."

"Wasn't you friends with Pauline Lunn?"

"So?"

"So she hates your guts."

"So?" I could see a sliver of freeway about a half a mile away with the squared yellow lights of cars and semi-tractor-trailers going by.

"She told Stew you shot him with your dead brother's gun. He's gonna kill you first war in June." An old man with a cowboy hat that looked like it was made out of chocolate came out of the store pushing a cart filled with pint bottles of Fresca to a Pontiac with the headlights on.

"So?" We watched the old man load his back-seat with bottles.

"So bang you're dead." She lit a cigarette and

played with the coin return while I drank a Coke leaning against the bricks. The old man's car started right up even though he'd left the lights on. He drove slowly to the dark end of the lot and his round red taillights disappeared on Rutledge.

"So why'd he dump you?" This didn't rile her at all, and she said " 'cause she's better than me." The parking lot was empty except for a couple of station wagons, one with a dog barking in it, and some banged-up shopping carts shining like birdcages under the bright lights.

She said, "What're you gonna do?"

"I don't know. What are you gonna do?" The pink parking lot lights buzzed and burned halos in the dark. It was going to storm soon.

"My dad's going to Wichita Falls soon to work. He found some job there. I'm goin' too. We're leaving next week." She flicked her cigarette into the parking lot and we watched it burn down to the filter.

Some thunder quietly rolled way to our left for nearly a minute. My Coke was sweating and dripped down to my elbow when I took a drink. "Where'd he get the gun?"

"It's a shotgun. From Eddy Tilton." Eddy lives a few streets away from me on Olvert Avenue. He dropped out of school and fixes cars. He's kind of slow. He gave me my first beer, a Balantine ale in a warm green can. He used to let me sit on a stack of Hemmingses in his garage and watch him pull black metal parts from car engines and explain them to me. He was with my brother George when he drowned and gets kind of quiet and tense when he talks about him, like a storm cloud—and I saw him break open and cry like one once too. "He got it for sixty bucks."

A bank of clouds lit up for a second. In one corner of the lot a couple of kids on bikes raced around for a second, then they were gone and the wind picked up where they were and stirred up some circles of dust and an empty bag of chips that climbed up in the sky and disappeared like a helium balloon.

"There's my dad." The brown Chevy pulled into the lot from Rutledge and drove straight at us and pulled alongside the curb. A heavy red face stared at us from the inside and Julie got in the backseat and rolled down the window, but didn't say anything. They drove off to the right, away from the storm, and I didn't watch them.

Another swirl of wind moved the shopping carts in the lot all at the same time, like a school of fish, when a fatter roll of thunder, which sounding like a stomping giant on the roof of the Value-Maxx, scared me a little and I braced to watch the storm. It was quiet for a minute, then the sky was flash after flash and crack after crack of thunder, but none of it seemed very close when rain started in drops, slapping cars and pavement like quarters. The dog in the station wagon stopped barking and looked at me for a second then ducked under the dash. The rain started falling harder, like somebody turning up the volume on an empty place on the radio dial. I saw a flash of lightning that looked like a birch tree in a book of pictures by Ansel Adams I saw once, and a second later the lights in the store and the parking lot went out, and I was standing there without even the glow of the red Coke machine next to me. I watched the storm in the light of the lightning light over the dead houses and listened to the rain. Inside the store was the weird green light of the emergency generator. The rain slowed. The dog started barking again. The lights went on again with a chuank sound; the red glow came back to the Coke machine, and I walked home on the wet grass of front lawns.

Now it's June 16th a little before midnight and the first war starts tomorrow. I'm at the lot now and the weeds are dark and wet and cool and move a little when the wind comes and swirls them some every few minutes. I'm trying to write this stuff down in a flowery notebook under a little flashlight on a keychain, but the light from it is a dim yellow and it's hard to see, even with the lights from the tire place next door that they leave on all night. Some things have happened since the night of that storm. Stew got a license and a car, a metal-colored Buick, and he drives it with Pauline's curls falling out of the passenger window. I don't see her much now except in that car. She looks at a place that feels like the hollow in my neck when she goes by and then drops her head back and laughs at the car ceiling as Stew steps on the gas and bends that silver monster around a corner out of sight. But sometimes I can see a glint of it through the houses on the block and it all looks the same, just a little safer and littler.

I dug a hole under the back fence, where I am now, just big enough to squeeze through when I'm through with all of this and I can bolt home without anybody seeing me. I'm wearing a dark shirt and jeans and old sneakers that I can throw in the drainage pipes on Denton street so no one will know my footprints, and I'll burn this book too, but I want the truth down somewhere for a little while, at least. The war starts at nine tomorrow officially, but I'm going to stay here all night until he shows up. I know he'll come early too. Last day of school was yesterday and nobody's been talking about his gun lately, like everybody forgot the whole thing, but I know Stew didn't forget and I bet he thinks I did. He thinks he's the coolest motherfucker with that black eyepatch, like he's glad his eye got shot out.

And me, I'm not going to wait till I'm seventeen. I'm going to get out soon and forget this business and take a Greyhound to Wichita Falls or maybe Nacogdoches and see Dad and who he's with now. I'll bet she's got money-colored tattoos on her ankles and he'll tell her to be sweet to me and we'll get along just fine and Dad will love us both more 'cause his girlfriend and his only living baby love each other so much, and maybe he'll be calm for a few months.

It's chilly here in the weeds and my hand aches a little from where I tore the webby part between my thumb and finger shooting this gun last week that I got from Eddy Tilton after he started crying about George again. I have a glove on and I should be able to shoot it all right, though. Now I can hear Stew's old car, it's about five blocks away. He's coming earlier than I thought. I wonder if Pauline's with him, too?

Killing Harvey

by N. C. Reynolds

L ee crushed out his cigarette and took another drink of black coffee.

"Cress, everyone is a witch," he said, brushing the cat's tail out of his face. Cressida kept a very loose rein on the animal, and it was constantly jumping up on the kitchen table and attempting to steal food off his plate. Fortunately, Lee was a vegetarian and the cat was usually less than interested in his food. But this morning he was eating cantaloupe and Rhiannon was taking dives for it every few seconds.

"Yes, I understand that, but what I am trying to tell you, and what I think is actually very important if we're going to pursue this relationship is that I am a *real* witch." Cressida swept her long black hair back over her shoulder.

Lee lit another cigarette.

"Meaning?" he asked.

"I can work magic," Cressida replied. "That's what 'witch' means."

"Real magic?"

"Absolutely."

"Hold that thought, Cress." Lee finished his coffee and went into the kitchen to get himself another cup, wincing at the pain his actions caused him. The previous day a pickup truck had plowed through a red light and smashed into his car, leaving his left leg bruised from ankle to thigh. When he returned to the table his cantaloupe and the cat were both missing.

He reseated himself and said, "So go ahead. Do that voodoo that you do so well."

"What do you mean? Here?" Cressida gestured around her dining room as if to suggest that the room itself was unworthy of the attention.

"Yeah," Lee replied. "Light a candle or something."

Cressida scowled. "I hate parlor tricks."

"Never mind, Cress. I believe that you can do magic, okay?"

"No, you don't."

"Sure I do." Lee smirked into his cup. "You

certainly managed to work some last night." It was then that his coffee cup vanished, leaving the coffee hanging for one impossible moment in the air before it splashed down on the table and into Lee's lap.

"I can't stand being smirked at," Cressida said.

Lee could only stare at her. He had known Cressida for only six months and had been sleeping with her for the last three weeks. He thought the woman slightly odd and enormously tacky, but never would he have guessed that a person of any magical ability whatsoever would be fond of wearing tiger-striped hot pants. It just didn't fit with the seriousness of sorcery in general.

"Do something else," Lee demanded, ignoring the hot coffee dripping off the table. Cressida smiled and held out her fist. Smoke was curling up through her knuckles. Suddenly she flipped her hand open, palm upward. Sitting neatly on Cressida's outstretched hand was Lee's coffee cup.

"But these are just tricks," Cressida insisted. "Nothing impressive. The important thing is this— I think I may have fallen in love with you, not that that means anything."

"What?!" Lee sat up straight.

"What I mean to say is that it's not the undoing of my power. *Au contraire*, it is an expression of the completeness of my skill."

"Are you saying that you cast a love spell on me?" Lee asked suspiciously.

"Just a little one," Cressida said. Secreted underneath the kitchen table, Rhiannon started to chew noisily on Lee's cantaloupe. "But it's all worked out now. It was just to get you to come home with me."

"I see."

"But anyway, the reason I'm telling you at all is that I think we might be head over heels in love." Cressida said this in the kind of dramatic, romantic way that made Lee want to dive for cover. "And just as I would tell you if I were some kind of crime lord or international spy, I feel like I should tell you that I'm a witch. A demon hunter."

Lee looked across the table at his lover, and then the pragmatic part of his mind simply took over. This often happened to Lee when he was trying to systematically reassess everything that he believed to be real and unreal about the universe. Before this morning he hadn't even considered the possibility that magic existed, now his girlfriend was making his coffee cups vanish at will. Behind his calm blue-green eyes Lee's mind was scrambling trying to cope, but his mouth simply took another casual drag off his Marlboro then said, "So do you have a coven?"

"I don't really work well in groups," Cressida replied, then took a bite of her breakfast, which consisted of a piece of chocolate cake, a diet cola, and a triple espresso.

"I thought witches were supposed to be in harmony with nature," Lee said, eyeing Cress's breakfast meaningfully.

"I am not a country witch," Cressida said. "I am most certainly a city witch. It would be ludicrous for me to go prancing around the apartment house lawn with a corn stalk wrapped around my head pretending to invoke the spirit of the harvest. Of course, it would be equally silly for me to go and be one with a traffic light, but that is beside the point."

"What is the point?" Lee asked. "Or did you just want to come clean with me about the witchiness?"

"I believe that they are aware of my connection with you."

"Who?"

"The demons. I think that one of them was driving the truck that hit you yesterday. You see, I am known to them, and they to me." Cressida stood up and began to pace back and forth under a line of dried herbs that hung from her dining room ceiling. "Normally I try not to make attachments for exactly this reason. But Lee, I do love you and, moreover, I think that you could help me."

"Help you what?"

"Hunt. You're a good fighter."

"Only in competition," Lee protested. He held a black belt in karate, and due to interesting circumstances in his childhood was also very good with knives, but he hadn't been in a real fight for years.

"And there's also your line of work." Cressida bit her lip and looked a little sheepish. "I'm aware of how you make money."

"How is that?" Lee asked, successfully maintaining an air of complete innocence.

"Burglary."

"Who told you that?"

"Rhiannon."

"You sent your cat to spy on me?" Lee said.

"What Rhiannon does in her free time is none of my concern," Cressida said. "But she decided to follow you and then told me because she thought that I needed to know. Please don't be upset, I don't care that you break into houses all the time. It's legitimate redistribution of wealth as far as I'm concerned, and I think what you do with the guns is very good as well."

Lee brooded over the woman's words. What Cress was referring to was Lee's habit of stealing handguns and burying them on the prairie about sixty miles out of town. Lee considered it his own method of gun control. Cress took another breath and barreled onward.

"So I'm almost certain that you and I were meant to be, being who we are and where we are." Cressida crossed the room to Lee, put her hands on his shoulders and smiled down on him. "We're destined to fight together. I'm sure of it, and I'm prepared to seduce you if it comes to that," Cressida finished, running her thumb along Lee's jaw. In concurrence with her mistress, Rhiannon hopped up on the table and started whiskering Lee's ear.

Lee was looking straight at Cressida's tank top, which was red and covered with sequins. Her pants were tight and black; a pair of cherry cowboy boots completed her chic ensemble. Lee had to remind himself that he had not been hallucinating when he'd seen Cress do her coffee cup trick.

"I have to think about it, Cress," he said, nudging Rhiannon's nose out of his ear.

"Will today be long enough?" Cress asked. "It's very important that I know. I'm hunting tomorrow, and I want to know if you'll be with me."

"Who exactly are you hunting?"

"Right now? Harvey."

"Harvey," Lee repeated.

"That's what he calls himself," Cressida said. "He pretends to drive a tow truck, but I've seen him kill."

"Are you sure that these guys aren't just serial killers?"

"I'm certain. They change, they conjure, they devour the flesh and souls of humans. If that's not a demon then I'm Marilyn Monroe." Cressida flipped her straight hair back over her shoulder.

Lee rested his hands on Cressida's waist. "How many of these tow truck drivers have you killed?"

Cressida didn't immediately answer. Instead she started to remove a wide black bracelet that she wore on her left wrist. Underneath it were a series of notched scars that went twice around her wrist.

"Twenty-three in all," Cressida answered. "Do you want to see their teeth?"

"Sure." Lee kept reassuring himself that Cressida had made a cup disappear and reappear with honest-to-god magic, but that wasn't dispelling the frightening notion that Cressida might be a crazed vigilante.

Cressida went into her bathroom and pulled a rubber box out from under the sink. From out of it she produced a string of long, yellow teeth. Rhiannon hissed at them and ran straight under the bed. Each of the fangs was about two inches long, and they stank like rotten cheese.

"You can put them away now," Lee said when he saw them and waved the smell away from his face.

Cressida replaced them, then came back to the dining room.

"I don't suppose you have decided whether or not to help me?" Cressida asked.

"Not yet. Where do these demons come from?"

"Well, as far as I can tell they come from Kansas. There's some kind of disturbance there where things come through. Amy says they chose Kansas because there are so few people. Amy is an associate of mine who lives in Dallas.

A few of us have noticed the larger number of demons in the U.S. and Canada. We think they might also be in Mexico, but who can tell down there? So many strange things happen anyway without any demonic involvement whatsoever."

"Do you know what they want?"

"No." Cressida shook her head. "They don't seem to be very smart individually, but they do seem to have objectives. Do you want some more coffee?"

"What? No, it's okay." Lee ran a hand through his spiky hair and regarded his lover thoughtfully. "I think I'll have to see one of these demons before I can agree to kill anyone."

"I understand completely," Cressida said. "But be careful. If you wait long enough they'll come to you."

Lee agreed to think about joining Cressida's crusade, but explained that he really did have to go and feed his dog. He then took his leave of Cressida's apartment, pausing only long enough for the woman to kiss him deeply and press a small cylindrical object into his hand.

"If the demon attacks you, throw this as high into the air as you can," Cressida told him, then closed the apartment door.

Lee went home, fed his dog, and tried to figure out what to do. He didn't have to wonder whether or not to believe Cress could do some magic; the disappearing coffee mug had taken care of that. And Cressida couldn't have known about Lee's job without some serious detective work. Lee looked around suspiciously for Rhiannon, but didn't see her anywhere.

What he couldn't deal with was the knowledge that Cressida was going around killing tow-truck drivers whom she believed to be flesh-eating demons. If they weren't really demons, what could Cress be thinking? Had she actually seen them eating people? And last, but certainly not least, why did he always get weirdo girlfriends? Lee sat down in the backyard and lit a cigarette.

He was thoughtfully smoking it when the doorbell rang. Lee went back inside to answer it. It wasn't until he had his hand on the doorknob that he felt something strange. It was the feeling he got when he was in the middle of a break and the lovely occupants of the home returned. It was the tingling sensation in his left palm that happened before he could hear or see danger.

He stepped back from the door.

The doorbell rang again.

He felt stupid, but he also couldn't bring himself to open the door.

Whoever it was who was outside started knocking.

Lee walked back to his kitchen and opened the refrigerator. He had three handguns in his vegetable drawer that he hadn't had the opportunity to bury yet and ammunition for each. He grabbed one of these, stuck it in big front pocket of his pants, then went back to the door.

The doorbell rang again.

Lee opened the door. It was the plumber. He had called the guy about his shower six days ago, then promptly forgotten he'd made the appointment. He smiled graciously, then led him to the bathroom and the offensive drip.

He sat down at the kitchen table and waited for the plumber to finish. His fingers clenched and unclenched around his still tingling palm. There was no way he could get it to stop, and it made him extremely nervous. Finally he wandered back into the bathroom to find out how the plumber was doing.

He wasn't doing anything. He was sitting on the toilet fondling a wrench.

"Excuse me." Lee shoved his hand into his pocket, and wrapped his hand around the butt of the revolver. "What are you doing?" Lee stepped backward sharply as the man looked up. He was much hairier than he had been before and his eyes were sunken and glittery.

"Nothin', " the man responded, his voice thick and sticky with mucus. He hefted the wrench in his hand then lumbered off the toilet seat toward Lee. He was fully three feet taller than he had been when Lee answered the door. The tattered remains of his plumber's shirt bore the name *Harvey* embroidered in red cursive letters.

Lee pulled out the gun, leveled it at Harvey, and pulled the trigger. Nothing happened, and Lee realized that the safety was on. He turned and tore down the hall. Harvey hurled the wrench at him. Lee staggered forward as it slammed into his back but kept going. He finally got the safety off, then spun and fired all six shots into Harvey's chest. The demon stopped, blinking in confusion at his mutilated chest.

Lee didn't bother to wait for him to understand what had happened. He ran into the kitchen, got the other two guns with their ammo, and ran out the back door into his yard. He made sure both guns were loaded and the safeties were firmly off, then waited. He could hear his dog whining underneath the steps, but didn't want to call attention to him. He didn't think Harvey would care about the dog.

A minute passed and nothing happened. Harvey didn't come outside, nor did he even make a sound. Maybe Harvey was dead. Lee reached into his pocket to get his cigarettes. As Lee reached in his fingers touched the small thing Cressida had given to him, presumably for just such an occasion as this. He held it up, trying to figure out what it actually was. It looked like a firecracker wrapped in red-and-white striped paper.

Lee glanced up at his house. There was still no sign of Harvey, so he started inspecting the fire-cracker again, stopping when his dog began to bark violently. Harvey was standing in the door-way looking furious. His chest was still mangled and bleeding, but it didn't seem to be inconveniencing him too much.

Lee threw the firecracker up and toward Harvey. When it reached its apex the little tube stopped. It hung in the air then started to spin, shooting out sparks in a twelve foot-radius and showering both Harvey and him. To Lee the sparks didn't feel like anything, but Harvey started to scream. He flung his hands over his eyes and whined horribly. Where the sparks hit his skin started to bubble. He tried to advance on Lee, but there were too many of the slivers of light hitting his already wounded chest. He ran back into the house and out the front door. Lee heard the tires on Harvey's van squealing on the pavement, then he was gone.

The shower of sparks turned bright red then fizzled out completely.

Lee sighed, turned around, and almost shot Cressida, who was standing directly behind him, the red sequins on her shirt glittering wildly in the afternoon sun.

"Well, I'd say that they definitely know that you're with me," Cressida commented. "Are you all right, my sweet?"

"Fine." Lee suddenly recognized the oddity of his situation. He was standing in his backyard holding a pistol. He looked around for his neighbors. Fortunately it was football time, and they were all inside shouting at their TV screens.

"Then why are you hunching over?" Cress asked.

"Oh, Harvey hit me in the back with a wrench. It's just bruised." Lee had, in the excitement, forgotten about it. He still wasn't in the mood to dwell on it, so he called his dog instead. Sam flatly refused to come out from under the steps. Eventually Lee gave up trying to coax him.

Cressida had gone inside and was banging around in his kitchen. Lee followed her, wondering what else she could have in store. Rhiannon was sitting on the kitchen counter, playing idly with the phone cord. The rest of the phone was completely disassembled and lying near the sink. Cress was stringing some of the components together with fine copper wire and bending it into the shape a pentagram.

She glanced up when Lee came in, flashed him

a smile, then went back to her work.

"So what are you making?" Lee asked, once he'd gotten a glass of iced tea and reloaded his gun.

"A battery," Cressida answered. "There's no use in going anywhere now, Harvey is going to be back. I'll just have to kill him here."

"How are you planning on doing that, exactly?" Lee had fired six shots into the monster and had done little more than make him blink.

"I'll explain in a minute. I just need to finish this." Cressida then filled Lee's sink with water and poured a whole container of salt into it. When it was full, she set her delicate sculpture of copper and transistors into the sink then grabbed Lee's blender and cut the cord off it. Before Lee could protest Cressida plugged the cord into the wall and dropped the frayed live wires into the water, which immediately began to bubble and steam.

"You're going to blow the house up!" Lee protested.

"I swear I'll buy you a new one." Cressida snaked her arms around Lee's neck, effectively preventing him from getting to the sink. "Just don't touch it until after the fight. Now let me look at your back." Cress kissed his cheek quickly then drew away.

Lee let Cressida look at his back, then made the witch sit down and talk. This in itself wasn't difficult. Cressida could speak at length about virtually anything. It was pinning her down to a topic, like Harvey or demons and the methods by which they can be killed, that was tough. When Cressida did finally come to demons the sky was beginning to darken.

"I take it, then, that you're going to join me in my cause?" Cress asked, seemingly unwilling to provide information to someone who wasn't a true believer. Even Rhiannon regarded him with dim suspicion, and a twitching tail.

"I'll kill Harvey," Lee responded guardedly. "You haven't defined your 'cause' well enough for me to fully commit to it."

"My cause is the extermination of demons!" Cressida said angrily, her cheeks flushed red. "You've seen Harvey. What more proof do you need?"

"I want to know where they come from, and what they're doing here," Lee replied in a reasonable tone.

"I don't know that!" Cressida's voice was strained. "I don't know what reason a virus has for killing either, but I'll still fight it."

"Well, then why are you even bothering waiting around to kill Harvey ? Why not go directly to the source?"

"Where? Kansas?"

"Beyond Kansas. To where they come from," Lee insisted.

"I don't know how to get there," Cressida admitted. "No one knows how to break across to the Hells. Amy has been trying, but . . ." She shook her head, trailing off into silence.

Lee was about to flatly refuse when he suddenly realized the logic inherent in Cressida's words. Harvey and his kind were real demons who had to be stopped right now. Cressida fought them alone and could use help. Later on he could figure out how to get 'across to the Hells,' or stop them from reaching Kansas at all.

"All right, Cress. I'll join you," Lee sighed. "Now will you please tell—"

Lee was cut off by Cress lunging across the room, throwing her arms around him and kissing him passionately. In fact, Cressida wouldn't stop kissing him. Normally Lee would have just taken this as a go ahead, but at the moment he was too nervous and shell-shocked to really get in the mood.

"Cress . . ." he began.

"I just knew you were the one." Cressida radiated waves of happiness. "Amy told me so, but I just couldn't have imagined—" She broke off to kiss him again, running her tongue lightly over Lee's mouth—"that it could begin to be true. So do you want to see my chains now?"

"Chains?" Lee repeated blankly. As Cressida leapt backward and rustled through her big black bag, Lee couldn't help wondering whether he would ever have the upper hand with her again. He somehow doubted it.

Cress had produced two spools of heavy link chain and was unwinding them across the living room. When they were finally unrolled each was about fifteen feet long, with a latch on one end and three vicious hooks on the other. Lee bent down to examine them more closely, reluctant to touch them because he had the idea that they would give him an electrical shock. When he finally picked up a length he could see that each link was etched with Cress's scratchy handwriting, but he couldn't read the words.

"I modeled the hooks after sharks' teeth." Cressida said proudly, removing a leather vest from the bag.

"What are the words?"

"Just spells, and charms. You know, 'Be sure and true,' 'Hold fast.' Things like that." Cressida laced on the vest, then attached each of the ends of the chain to rings on her shoulders. "I catch Harvey with these, and hold him. You're going to have to kill him."

"With what?"

Cressida looked doubtful for a moment. "I thought you had guns."

"I do, but what do you normally use?"

"A rending spell, but I don't think you can do one of those," Cressida said.

"What's a rending spell?"

"A spell that pulls its head off. They're very effective for stunning it, but a demon can still live without its head. The trick is to get his heart out before he reanimates. That you have to use this for." Cressida delved into her bag again.

"Just let me get some ammo first," Lee said, holding up a hand to stay Cressida's movements.

"Okay, I'll find it in a second." Cress was pulling everything out of her bag and spreading the stuff on the carpet. There was a pair of pliers and a small saw. There was also a tube of lipstick, some sunglasses, and a jingle bell on the floor when Lee departed for the kitchen.

He set out a bowl of food for Sam and set about loading all three guns. He was trying to figure out what to use for holsters when there was a huge thud and the crack of a splintering doorframe.

"Lee!" Cressida screamed, her voice shrill with adrenaline.

In an instant, Lee was on his feet and bolting for the kitchen door. He kicked the door open and then stopped, for the smallest instant stunned by the tableau before him. Harvey was looming huge and hairy in the doorway. Cressida was standing and holding the hooked ends of the chain in her hands, a pair of heavy leather gloves that she hadn't had a chance to put on at her feet, and she was slowly beginning to glow. Her hair was already standing straight on end, electric blue sparks snapping at the air around it. The chains were also glowing dark red and scorching the carpet where they touched. The whole room was filled with the hum of electricity, and it seemed that this momentarily disoriented Harvey.

"Hold your fire!" Cressida shouted, then started to back down the hall.

Harvey caught her movement and lunged after her, his arms held out stiff. Cressida let one of the chains fly. It wrapped around Harvey and embedded itself wetly in his shoulder. Harvey shrieked like steel on a blackboard and jerked at the chain. The motion sent Cressida hurtling into and through a plasterboard wall. With Cress out of the way Lee fired and blasted a hole through Harvey's only partially healed chest.

"You hurt me," he said to Lee in a thick voice.

Lee didn't know what to say and fired again, but Harvey dodged the bullet.

Cress staggered out seconds later, covered in white dust. Blood was pouring from the side of her head. Harvey pulled on the chain again, but Cress braced herself and threw the other chain. It pierced Harvey's thigh. He thrashed wildly, slamming Cress back and forth, but with supernatural strength the witch held her ground, and held Harvey as well. The chains were glowing golden now; Lee could smell the hot metal from across the room.

Suddenly Harvey stopped. A new idea had entered his mind. He started to pull Cressida toward him.

"Lee?!" Cressida pulled backwards with all her might but was still dragged forward. "Now!" Cressida dropped to the floor out of the line of fire. Lee jumped forward just as Harvey turned. The muzzle of the gun was right at his forehead when Lee pulled the trigger, splattering the entire top of Harvey's head across the ceiling.

As the demon crumpled, Cressida rolled out of the way of his body. Lee rushed forward, sickened by the sight of Harvey's chest still regularly rising and falling, and without sight or scent his arms still flailing for something to grab.

"My bag." Cressida gestured toward her forgotten bag. Her hands were blistered from the heat
and she looked ghastly. Lee rushed forward and
grabbed it for her. There was only one thing left in
it, a sheathed dagger. Lee got the buckles undone
and removed the shiny blade. He turned back and
saw Cressida frantically unlacing her vest, trying
to disengage from Harvey, who was pulling himself to his feet.

Lee kicked him hard in the knee, feeling his
tendons tear, and he fell back down again.

"Into the chest! Hurry, please," Cressida said
sweetly. She had slipped out of the vest and was
now standing over Harvey. She held her red hands
in the air over his chest, moving them as if she were
ripping the space beneath her palms apart. Lee
ducked to avoid Harvey's flailing arm, then
stabbed the dagger into Harvey's breastbone.

The point of the dagger easily sliced into the
monster's chest, then suddenly the entire chest
cavity exploded open.

"Get his heart," Cressida gasped. Her hands
were apart now, as if she were holding the ribs
open. Lee didn't waste time. He saw the rib cage
flex as Harvey tried to close his wound, but
Cressida held it open. Lee went straight for his
heart. Even when he cut it out it was still pump-
ing, but Harvey ceased to move.

Cressida sagged against the wall, drenched in
sweat and shaking with exertion and injury.

"Here," Lee said. Cressida held out her hands,
and Lee dropped the obscenely writhing organ into

them. Cressida walked to the kitchen and dropped it into the frothing and electrified sink, where it convulsed, then finally stopped.

"I really wasn't expecting him to come so soon. But you were brilliant," Cressida sighed adoringly, "Let me see your arm." Lee held out his arm. Cressida wearily grabbed the dagger out of her other hand then cut a small nick in Lee's arm, one in her own, and collapsed into a dead faint on the kitchen floor.

Lee picked her up and carried her to the car. He noted, as he went by, that where Harvey's headless body lay there was only a disintegrating pile of slick membranes, which Rhiannon was standing sentinel over.

Lee rounded up Sam, caught Rhiannon, and propped the door up so that it looked reasonably closed from the street, then drove to the nearest hotel and checked in. The desk clerk didn't even bother to look up at as he handed Lee the keys.

"Have a good night, sir," he mumbled, and went back to reading *Playboy*.

"You, too," Lee replied tiredly. "Do you have room service?"

"Sure do." The man looked up for the first time. His eyes widened at Lee's bloody visage.

"Well, then, I want a dozen roses and a map of Kansas delivered to my room tomorrow morning." Lee thought a moment. "And some chocolates."

"In the morning, sir?"

"First thing." Lee smiled slightly, then walked

back to his car.

To his relief Sam and Rhiannon simply followed him as he carried Cressida to the room. He gently laid her down on the bed. He took a shower without waking her, though the witch's eyes fluttered open when Lee switched on the TV.

"Lee?" she whispered.

"Right here." He reached out and stroked her hair away from her face.

"Come to bed, my sweet." Without bothering to move, Cress turned off both the TV and the lights. Lee laughed into the quiet darkness, then acquiesced.

"You could come in pretty handy," he murmured, curling his arm around Cressida's body.

"Thank you." Cressida snuggled closer to him. "You could, too."

Lee fell asleep, thinking of Kansas.

Blanco y Negro

by Thomas Cooney

I

She is easy to spot—the only person sitting at the outside tables at Berysa. It is one o'clock and most of the residents of Salamanca are home finishing their lunches and preparing for their siestas. But she is not a resident. Neither is he.

Kevin walks slowly across the wide, quiet and somber Plaza Mayor where Nadine is waiting for him. In his hand he holds a box of chocolates and her note. From across the plaza he can easily see how her faded face is on the verge of completely disappearing. She is not the same person he met three weeks earlier.

"Looking for the frog?"

Kevin had been sitting on a bench outside the registration center for a few minutes when the woman approached him.

He looked up. Her long, light brown hair fell over her shoulders and dangled between her and Kevin. Her face was tan, her freckles numerous and proud.

"What frog?"

She sat down next to him on the cool stone bench. "The frog of the facade, of course." She pointed to an intricate, three-tiered, sand-colored frieze above a university doorway.

Kevin put his pen down and walked over to get a closer look. In the center of the facade was the university seal; below that, portraits of Isabella and Ferdinand. There were saints, winged figures, snakes, flowers—"I'm supposed to find a frog here?"—vases, dragons, anonymous portraits—"It's part of the myth"—shells, crowns, wreaths, crosses, cherubs.

Kevin stumbled back to the bench, feigning dizziness. A cool wind began to cut through the hot afternoon. "I'm supposed to find a frog among all that?" he asked again.

"Yep. And if you do, it means you'll return to Salamanca one day," she said, slowly brushing her hair from her eyes and mouth.

"How long do I get to look for it?"

She laughed, he thought, at him. "For how-ever long you're here. I found it in my second week, back in '85."

"You were here before?"

"On a summer program just like this one. The frog brought me back. My name's Nadine Sawyer."

He held out his hand. "Kevin Bessner."

"How old are you, Kevin Bessner?"

"Nineteen." He didn't return the question for he could see that behind the dark complexion, the obvious freckles, the long hair and exuberance, she was easily past thirty.

"Let's say we go to Berysa for a drink?" she offered.

"I'm not sure I know what that is," he said, openly, without embarrassment, already feeling comfortable with her.

"It's the best bar in the Plaza Mayor," she explained with a travel-agent authority. She took him by the hand and pulled him off the bench.

Berysa was one of the many bars that ran along the colonnade of the sprawling Plaza Mayor. The strong sun sent waves of heat flickering in the distance between their table and the dull gold walls. "What'll you have?" Nadine asked.

"A Coke," Kevin said automatically.

"Hmm," she scolded, as the waiter walked over to their table. "I'll allow it just this once, but from here on out you'll have to abandon those American drinks."

"Well what *should* I have?"

"Stay with the Coke, you look a little homesick. *I*," she remarked with great pride, as though it were a special occasion that had to be met with a special drink, a drink to which she was entitled, "*I* am going to have a *Blanco y Negro*."

"Which is?"

"You'll see."

The waiter soon returned and quickly popped the cap off the Coke bottle, letting the metal disc clank onto the pavement, then placed a cup of coffee and a tall glass with only a scoop of vanilla ice cream in front of Nadine. The waiter slipped a small register receipt on the tablecloth and left. Nadine poured the coffee on the ice cream and held the glass up to Kevin. The sun caught the mixing of the colors. "*This* is a *Blanco y Negro*." They both watched the two colors meet like enemies, like distant cultures. The strong black sliced through the melting white. Trails of cream swam upward through the heavy dark coffee, twirling and spinning before joining in a marbled brown. In a matter of seconds the entire melange turned a rich, dense hue somewhere between tan and leather.

It was odd how the scent of exhaust fumes, improper sewer channeling, and cooking oils, which now waft in concert past his face as he walks across the Plaza Mayor, reminds him of how attached he has become to Salamanca. When he sits next to Nadine, and before handing her the box of chocolates, he sees that she is trying to hide her gauze-wrapped right hand in her left armpit.

They had seen each other daily during the initial week. "How's class?" Nadine had asked on their first Friday afternoon. "You've had a week, what do you think?"

"Kind of difficult."

"Supposed to be," she said, sipping at her beer. "Go on."

"I don't know. It's coming along, I guess. I've met a few people. In fact, we're all going to a disco tonight. Want to come?"

"Which one?"

"Tito's." He called the waiter over for another round of beers. The high sun had made the day far too hot for anything else.

"I've already been, you go ahead. But don't get carried away with partying. You'll lose sight of what really matters here."

"Like?"

She thanked him for the beer and looked around the plaza. "The dry, cobblestoned, mostly treeless streets and alleys winding around all the university buildings. You know, this is one of the oldest universities in the world, and certainly the most prestigious in Spain. Cervantes studied here, don't forget." She ran her fingers around her neck as if to locate and tighten any sagging skin. "Spend your summer the Spanish way—spend time with your *familia*, go to church on Sundays with them; never, *never* go to the Burger King, brought in, I'm sure, by too many American students' demands and complaints; buy a lottery ticket once a week—"

"What about bullfights? Shouldn't I see a bull-fight?"

"No. If you ever get to Portugal, see one there. They don't kill the bull in their version." She paused and shielded her eyes with sunglasses. "I try to minimize the cruelty I have to see," she added, and Kevin understood. It made perfect sense to him.

Nadine touched his hand and continued. "You should also try to spend at least three hours a day here at Berysa, and you'll want to buy leather goods and Toledo silver for gifts back home. Take siestas, and don't be afraid of the sun—it brings out beauty." She flicked back her hair as if on cue to show more of her face. "And mostly, appreciate this town's love of family. I've never seen anything quite like it."

The word *family* slapped him across the face, a stinging reminder of home. Home: the reason he went through his days like a well-trained prize-fighter who protects himself by leaving no open-ings of his own and exposing any open hole he might find in the lives of others.

He looked up at the clouds. Thin white trails hovered under an ice-blue sky.

"This is what they call a Velazquez sky," Nadine said. "Yet another thing to appreciate about this town."

Nadine looks over at him as soon as he sits down. She doesn't speak a word.

"How's your hand?"

She looks in the direction of the hand rather than bringing it out from the safety of the armpit.

"I got your note," he says with a sense of shame and failure. That is the problem with him—he absorbs the pains and disappointments of others. But he has no choice, he feels. It is either to absorb their pains or let them in on his.

"I wanted to see you before I left . . . I don't care about the others," Nadine says, and then waves the waiter over to the table. "*Una cerveza y*—"

"*Blanco y Negro,* " Kevin adds.

"I wonder if you would have discovered that drink if it weren't for me."

"Probably not," he says.

She has not removed her sunglasses, and Kevin thinks that she probably believes they offer her some sort of protection, some guarantee of anonymity should she be spotted by anyone other than he.

Nadine doesn't have any luggage with her, and it is on her face, even more than in her note, that Kevin reads departure. "All packed?" he asks.

"Yep."

"What time does your train leave for Madrid?"

"Midnight—the hour of escape for gypsies, carnivals, and lonely women."

"You must really be having fun," she had said back in the middle of the second week. "I don't see you much anymore."

Kevin smiled and shook his head slowly from
side to side. "Well, why won't you ever come out
with us?" She had lost her brightness, Kevin
thought. Her face seemed bleached. Drab, dull, flat,
anonymous, dim. Sometimes she would stop looking at him when they spoke. Her eyes would just
drift off in some other direction.

"I'm too old to run around with sorority sisters looking for wet T-shirt contests." She had a
smirk on her face, as though she had found a
description for the group she called his "new
friends."

"It's not like that. How would you know anyway? You've never talked to any of them."

"I've met them."

"And that's enough?"

They were silent for what seemed to Kevin an
uncomfortably long time. Sitting next to him, the
hot desert wind blowing her ash-brown hair, shal-
low pools of beer in two tall glasses, the north and
east walls of the Plaza Mayor orange in the sun,
the blind lottery ticket-vendor under the plaza
colonnade shouting *"Buena suerte para hoy,"* the
shop awnings around the plaza falling gently as
the owners reeled them in for siesta time, Nadine
finally leaned over and said, simply, "I should
never have come back."

"Why?" Kevin asked. He felt a closeness, a
safety with her as he always did with others who
seemed to be burdened with some hidden regret.
He needed her there. His other friends were too
obsessed with superficial things like discos and

cheap beer and quick sex. When they talked of life back in the States, they talked of convertible cars, family incomes, preferred clothing. They never spoke of any misery or misfortune the way Nadine had. Kevin knew he could not feed off of their lives because their lives were not yet complete; there was no trace of pain or grief. He needed Nadine and her suffering, which he was always glad to share so long as he wouldn't ever have to tell her that he had lied when he told her his parents were still married. He would never tell her that he had really come to Spain to be away from the final stages of an ugly divorce between two people who couldn't realize that when they claimed to have never loved the other, they in a sense claimed to have never loved their only child. And so when Nadine said "I should never have come back," a low outrage inside Kevin prompted him to repeat his question, "Why do you say that?"

Nadine leaned back on the orange plastic chair and looked into Kevin's eyes. "I know what you're thinking. What could be wrong in this good, great place? I've only told you bits and pieces of my association with Salamanca. You see, when I was here before, I fell in love." She finished her beer and placed the tall glass on the table, which was covered with a brown, orange, and white checked plastic tablecloth. She made a disgusted face and looked at the glass. "Blaaach, warm."

"Who'd you fall in love with?"

"His name was Matthew Seymour. We met in class. He was from New York. Taught school." Her sentences were short utterances, as though she were spitting them out. They were protests, Kevin thought.

"It felt like a perfect match; it was like fate. I mean, what else could it have been? And then when we each found out that the other was a schoolteacher . . . I don't know, it just clicked. Funny thing is, I wasn't looking for someone." She paused for a minute as if weighing the advantages and disadvantages of her disclosures. "My boy-friend had committed suicide ten months earlier, and I looked at Spain as an escape." She stopped talking and looked directly into Kevin's eyes. "I'll tell you anything, but please don't ask about the suicide, please."

"Of course."

"Well, then I met Matthew. Every day we would come to Berysa—which is why I know the waiters so well. We were like a couple, you know? And then when we got back to the States we saw each other only twice. He kept coming up with excuses every time he canceled our plans. Don't ask me why. I suppose if I knew, I wouldn't be back here. Maybe New York City, with all that noise," and then she screamed, "WITH ALL THAT NOISE!" People looked at her, a waiter ran over to see if there was a problem. Nadine didn't no-tice. "Maybe New York City just swallowed him up when he returned." And then she stopped and looked around. "Pull over another chair," she said to Kevin, "he should be here any minute."

"Who?"

"Matthew."

"He's here?"

"Of course."

Kevin waited, silently. Nadine repeatedly looked over her left shoulder and her right shoulder. Her crimson fingernails tapped constantly on the metal frame of her chair. She didn't say anything for over five minutes.

"There were these two old men," she finally said, "who always sat in that table over there under the arch. They would come out after siesta and play a little game." Kevin noticed that she had stopped looking for Matthew.

"Have you had a lemonade here yet?" she asked.

"No, why?"

"Well, it's nothing more than fresh squeezed lemons, and when you order it the waiter brings it with a bowl of sugar, and you add whatever you need. So these two old men would start their afternoons off with a lemonade each, and they would challenge each other to see who could drink the whole glass of lemonade with the least amount of sugar." Kevin couldn't believe how fast Nadine was talking. The words just kept accelerating, and he had to do his best to keep up. "I suppose the quality of their lunches and siestas had a lot to do with how much sourness they could tolerate. And then they would spend a good two or three hours discussing politics, mainly Franco. Before they left, the challenge would be reversed. They would try to see who could drink a cup of coffee with the

most amount of sugar. Once Matthew and I saw
one of them put in twenty-six spoonfuls of sugar.
Neither one had many teeth," she said with a quiet
but, Kevin thought, good, necessary laugh.

"Have you seen them yet this summer?"

"No."

"Why don't you ask one of the waiters?"

"I'm afraid, I guess. They were both very old.
I'd like to just imagine that I keep missing them;
that maybe they've been taking their siestas at odd
times. . . . Well," she said, "speaking of siestas, I
guess it's almost time to go grab one."

And suddenly Kevin realized that Matthew
had never shown. "Was Matthew supposed to
arrive today?"

She shot a glare at him that read betrayal. A
look that also wondered if he were mocking her.
"I don't know what you mean. Matthew was here
four years ago. Why would you ask me that?"
Kevin apologized; he didn't know what he was
thinking, he said. And then he looked at Nadine
for a brief, quiet moment. She had a natural type
of attractiveness. The sun played nicely on her
round freckled face. He felt wronged. He decided
then that madness did not suit her; that madness
was for women in outfits too young for their age,
women with faces madeup like modern art portraits, women with dyed black hair, smeared red
lipstick, and painted-on moles. He refused to ac-
knowledge the streaks of madness displayed on the
kind face of a friend.

The next day Kevin waited for more than twenty minutes and Nadine did not come. He stood up from the table, paid for the beer, and headed toward her place. He clenched a fist when he walked past the Burger King, loathing it because it was like divorce—tasteless, cheap, unwholesome, and a leading American export. And, even more, he hated it because, even though it had already been there two years, it seemed to follow him to Salamanca.

He arrived at Nadine's apartment. He knocked on the door and didn't like the pity he felt for Nadine, who was staying with the same Señora she had stayed with four years ago. There was danger in her attempt to re-create everything, her attempt to glue back together a shattered Lalique.

A stout woman answered the door, a knife in her hand. Diced shards of garlic and green onions dangled from the blade. "*Si?*" She smiled. Her teeth—two gold-capped, one discolored to yellow, and one black and looking as though it might fall out right then—made her smile look like a row of Indian corn.

"*Puedo hablar con la Senorita Nadine?*"

Strands of silver and strands of black tumbled from her unsuccessful bun. "Aay," she said and for a moment covered her mouth. She began to wave the knife all around, and then looked down at the shining blade. "*Desculpe pero estaba haciendo gazpacho.*" She put the knife somewhere behind the door and out of Kevin's view. Kevin grew nervous. Something had happened to Nadine.

The woman leaned forward and said, being slow and careful with each word. *"Ella tuvo que ir al hospital. Se quemo la mano."*

"Donde esta?"

She leaned out of the doorway and held her hand over her eyes like a visor. She pointed to the west and all Kevin could catch was *derecha*. He thanked her, said good-bye, and headed in the direction, reminding himself to turn right at the end of the street.

When he entered the hospital room, his heart beating fast, Nadine was seated on a table and a doctor had just begun dressing the wound on top of her right hand. Kevin held his own right hand, feeling equal the pain in the way that Saint Teresa of Avila was said to be in agony when staring too long at the crucifix.

"What happened?"

Nadine looked down at the ground and shook her head. "I had an itch on my hand. It wouldn't go away."

Kevin could see the ointment glistening like a glass cover over her raw pink skin. "But that's not all, is it?"

"It just wouldn't stop, so I boiled some water and poured about a gallon over the itch." She started to cry and the doctor looked up and apologized, saying he didn't mean to hurt her. "I have to go home, Kevin, I can't stay here." Kevin knew she meant America. She was in too much pain for him to argue. He would just have to accept it: his cover had deteriorated and was about to leave him alone and vulnerable. He knew that if he took this moment to tell Nadine about his own pains and shame, then she might stay in Salamanca. But he couldn't do that for one bitter reason: Daniel Steuben, his best friend from junior high.

On the first day of tenth grade Daniel had approached Kevin during lunch hour and said, "Kevin, my folks are getting divorced." No matter how many phone calls Kevin made after that, no matter how many times he stopped by Daniel's house or no matter how many times he found him at school, Daniel never spoke to Kevin again. Ever since then Kevin feared whatever it was that was secreted when Daniel had said that one sentence.

"*Gracias*, Ramon," Nadine says as the waiter sets down their drinks. She reaches into her purse with her gauzed right hand and retrieves an un-opened pack of cigarettes, the sun temporarily reflecting off the cellophane and shining into Kevin's eyes.

"I didn't know you smoked."

"I just picked these up a few minutes ago. I always have a cigarette when I'm about to face failure," she says matter-of-factly, as if it was in-deed a ritual for her.

"Nadine . . . failure only comes if the task is easy."

She laughs, throaty and difficult; he knows it's the last emotion she wants at that moment. "Did I show you my ring?" she asks, jutting out her hand.

"New?" Kevin says, more concerned with her

hand, which has become as pale and pasty as the rest of her.

"Just bought it," she says as she takes off her sunglasses. Kevin notices that her problem has gotten worse. She used to be able to suppress her nervous eyes, but she no longer seemed to have control over them. They swirl, dip, and sink—they do everything but look straight at him.

"I figured with my university refund and the money I'll save by flying home early, I could easily afford it." She takes the ring off her right middle finger and shows it to him. A small diamond standing high on a silver setting. As he looks down at the ring, he senses the constant, restless movement of her eyes.

"Silver?"

She nods. "From Toledo." She puts her sunglasses back on. "A married woman wears gold," she adds, frankly, without bitterness, as if instructing her younger friend on her own certain rules of etiquette. And immediately, and for a short while (because he has come to believe that hesitation is a trait of the weak), he thinks of marriage and the happiness his parents now deny they ever had, thinks of the divorce and shame he hides from others, including Nadine.

"I'm sure your mother wears gold," Nadine says, trying to further her point.

"Yep." This is what one must do, he thinks, to retain a semblance of normalcy. One must just go along with the lies already laid down.

"I brought you a box of chocolates for your

train ride," Kevin says as he hands her the silver box, wrapped in a red ribbon that is too bright for the mood.

"Thank you, I know I'll enjoy them." Her response is civil, polite, as though any real emotion, good or bad, will send her over the edge without chance for rescue.

Two days after her "accident," her protest, her complaint against life, Nadine left a note for Kevin. When he returned from class for lunch, his Senora handed it to him:

Dear Kevin,

I'm leaving Salamanca tonight to go home.
I'd like to meet you in the Plaza at two. Please come.

Nadine

I'm really glad you could make it," she says as they enter their second hour at Berysa.

He smiles at her. "Wouldn't miss it for the world."

"It's our last day together," she says, and then sucks in some air and places a palm against her throat. Kevin wonders if she had said those same words to Matthew on their last day in Spain four years earlier.

She quickly recovers and says, "I imagine you'll have a great time the rest of the summer . . . especially with me out of the way."

"Nadine—"

"I'm sorry, that's just the way it is. I'm not saying you'll be glad to get rid of me, just that it's going to be easier on you without me. The burden will be gone."

And Kevin knows that what she is saying is, in a way, true. Nadine had no use for his friends. No matter how hard he tried, his notion of a "group" never got off the ground so long as there was Nadine—it seemed everyone he met never became more than just a name to her. And in the bright, clear days of the Spanish summer, it was very easy to see that to many of his friends, Nadine did not fit. But Kevin tried to mediate. Give her a chance, he would tell them. Don't seem so brooding, he would tell her. But the rift kept expanding.

Nadine became sarcastic and biting. And, just to bother them, she would join them when they came to Berysa and would sit slightly on the outside. She would sit there and drink a beer or a *Blanco y Negro*, depending on the weather. It became a game soon enough, and Kevin's allegiance was always torn. His other friends wanted to go to nightclubs and discos. Nadine, however, insisted on spending her time at Berysa. Sometimes she would claim that it was the best place to relax in the whole town, and on her bad days she said she couldn't leave, that she had to wait for Matthew. "He'd never forgive me if I wasn't here to greet him," she said once.

"Well," Kevin begins to say, "I know one thing—I won't have anyone to drink *Blanco y*

*Negro*s with."

"That's true. You could return to Coca-Cola with *los Americanos*," she says, taking a quick shot at his friends.

"But I can always get Coke in the States."

"A *Blanco y Negro* isn't a difficult order back in the States, either."

"Ah, but would it taste the same?" Kevin asks.

"Probably not. I haven't tried it. I've been afraid it'd be too bitter."

"Like the lemonade?"

She smiles and strokes his forearm softly. "Yes, like the lemonade."

The sun begins to fade over the west wall of the Plaza Mayor and all that is left is a ray or two of orange light on the east wall. The shops and markets around the square begin opening their doors and the city begins to wake up in time to lead the second half of the day into night. Small children run through the wide plaza with the energy that only a siesta could give them. Kevin and Nadine had always adhered to siesta times, except for this one day.

Nadine looks at her watch. "I've got to pack soon."

"But you told me you were already packed."

Nadine takes a deep breath and lowers her head. By now she openly accepts her lapses. "I don't know why I would have said that, because I'm not packed. I don't know, Kevin, I just don't know. One minute I'm fine, and the next minute I'm saying wrong things."

"Nothing's been easy for you here, Nadine," he says and puts his arm around her shoulder.

"Sometimes I thought I had it under control, and then out of nowhere I'd think it was four years ago. Everything is so timeless here . . . the waiters are all the same, the shops are all the same, the blind lottery-ticket man, everything."

"Except the old men with the lemonades."

"That's true, but still, that's not enough change. I wanted to come to a different city!" She slams her fist on the metal table.

"Then you should have gone to a different city!" Kevin challenges.

"But I can't associate Matthew with any other city."

"So then dis-associate him with this city."

"Can't you see that's what I'm trying to do. I'm trying to get my life back!"

Nadine slumps in her chair, then leans forward again. "So many of us live our lives like barterers—trading one moment for another, this moment for that moment. Well, what happens to those of us who can't play the game that way?" She stands up from the table, picks up her purse, and touches his hand. "Good-bye, Kevin. I wish there was more to say. I don't think we should exchange addresses or anything. I've tried that before, it doesn't work. Good-bye," She leans down and Kevin feels the warm plastic from her sunglasses as she kisses his cheek.

Behind him Nadine walks away. A few seconds later Kevin jumps out of his chair. If she's still there he'll run after her and tell her his secret, his dream to recover the past, to seal the past, to reclaim a life. But all he sees are strangers going about their way in the city square. Nadine is nowhere.

I I

"Kevin, Kevin," Susan Reid says, shaking him by the shoulders.

"Huh?" Kevin answers.

"You've gotta get up!"

Kevin sits up and looks at his watch—10:30. "I just went to sleep," he complains. "How'd you get in here?"

"Your Señora. You've got to come to the plaza."

"Why?"

"It's Nadine," she says with a hint of distaste.

"Is she all right?" he asks as pulls a fresh shirt from his suitcase.

"I don't know. Brian told me to come get you. Just hurry." Susan is from California, and, like the others, never warmed up to Nadine. They never understood what Kevin was doing hanging around with someone almost twice his age. He could have said sympathy, but that would have been unfair to Nadine, and he could have said he enjoyed her company, but he knew they would never have understood or believed that.

Kevin's apartment on San Justo was only a three-minute walk from the Plaza Mayor. When he and Susan are a block away they faintly see the light from the plaza rise some feet into the air, like flames lighting up a night sky. On weekends when clowns, jugglers, fire-eaters, and mimes occupied the plaza, the light would be so bright that it seemed like daytime. But this is only a weeknight, and they will have to settle for what light there is.

In the middle of the plaza, centered by four lampposts, a small crowd has gathered. Kevin approaches the crowd nervously, not knowing in what sort of cruel position he might find Nadine.

As he makes his way through the onlookers he hears nothing. And then above the heads of the people in the first row he sees Nadine's hands hanging limp at the wrist. He pushes his way to the front and sees her with her arms above her head, dancing slowly in a circle, the eyes of her faded, faded face closed. He also notices she has removed the gauze from her hand. The lights from the lamps make a blurry reflection on the protective ointment that covers the deep red lesion.

For a moment she opens her eyes, and Kevin knows it's his opportunity to jump in and pull her aside, grab her luggage and get her to the train station. But instead Kevin stands there, like all the others, and watches her dance. He watches her solitary El Greco figure move clumsily without rhythm or grace. He watches Nadine dance in that plaza whose walls display statues of cherubs and turn orange at sunset, above whose arches are apartments with iron-railed balconies. She is dancing in that city of blue skies, narrow streets, multicolored awnings, tiled roofs, churches, statues, cathedrals, handicapped civil war veterans, families, *Blanco y Negros*, courtyards, and dramatic lamp posts. Nadine is dancing, not slow, not fast, and without any music; and, Kevin thinks, in that city and in that plaza that on weekends houses carnival performers, it just seems so right and fair and just.

Kevin realizes that his other friends had called on him to stop her, to rescue her from shaming herself any further. But he doesn't see it like that. He isn't going to step into her dancing ring and pull her away. He would rather just stand there and envy her, knowing that she has a train to which she can escape.

Bard's Call

by Honore Hillman Foster

C ormac watched her with eyes lit by moon-
light, one hand on the hilt of his sword in
his familiar gesture. Shadows shifted and blurred
across his face, making his expression unreadable,
but his eyes said it all. Kerensa froze, her mouth
going dry, while around them the night deepened
and a breeze woke a song in the trees overhead.
All the defenses she had built quivered, suddenly
fragile. Fear rolled through her one final time and
subsided, replaced by an emotion she did not at

first recognize, one that swelled and burst through her like a thousand stars. She had, she understood then, been waiting for this since the first time she had seen him, more than a year ago, standing aloof and withdrawn, forever apart. He, like herself, bore the shadow-scars of great pain, not quite healed, and his pain called to her, irresistible and inexorable. Behind her, she knew, the empty tent showed a wedge of darkness where the flap had been tied back to permit the sweet night air to circulate within. That dark openness drew her, frightened her.

They might have been alone in the encampment.

He moved, just enough to free his hand from its grip on the top of the sword hilt. Then he extended the hand to her. The gesture in itself was simple enough, but she saw the faint tremble of light across it and knew what effort it cost him.

"Are you asking, then?" And she did not recognize her voice.

"I am." The tone was quiet.

She felt the need in him, knew it to be matched by her own, and knew, too, that he was aware of it. "There will be no going back," she challenged, and he nodded.

"No."

"I am Kindred, a FullRank Bard."

"Yes. I am StarSworn. And death could be waiting for one or both of us, tomorrow."

"I know, Cormac. Let tomorrow bring what it will." She stepped aside, motioned for him to enter the tent. The flap fell closed behind him, shutting out the night. He made a quick gesture and a blue ball of light appeared, sending a soft radiance to enclose them, then unbuckled his sword belt and laid it aside. Once again he held out his hand. This time she took it.

His hand bore callouses and scars, the signatures of his profession. It closed around her own with a warmth, a joining of more than hands. He pulled her to him, bent his mouth to hers.

Deep in her something woke, a wild fury of desire welling up from what had always been frozen depths. She opened her mind then, sending out a shy tendril to his, and shuddered as it was enveloped in a searing response.

Never before had he opened himself to anyone as he had to her, not once since a confused frightened child had been torn away from his sobbing mother and taken away to learn to become . . . She wanted to cry at what had been done to him. His mind touch altered, became wary, even as the pressure of his mouth against hers changed.

No! she cried. *No! Don't judge me by that! That was in the past!* And she sent him her innermost reactions to the gift of his trust.

He groaned, the sound deep in his chest, and his mouth slid from hers to her throat, trailing fire as it moved downward. She arched against him, obeying an instinct never before acknowledged. Her hands slipped up to his hair to bury themselves in the thick glossy black strands, glorying in the texture of it. His hands moved, and the urgency in his kisses grew. So long dormant, needs filled her with such force that she wanted him now, wanted the gentleness to change into a match for the inferno that burned within.

Without warning, panic slapped at her. She pushed free of the intimacy of his embrace, stiffening as his arms became something else, a nightmare of helplessness and degradation. From the deep, buried well of her childhood poured forth the memories of why she had closed herself off to all sexual encounters. Falling to her knees, she felt the long-ago pain rise up with a terrifying suddenness. She saw the understanding in his eyes as he looked down at her and quivered as the tension ebbed, so she could, for the first time, see it clearly.

What? he asked her then, easing down on the sleeping furs across from her, the words gentle. *Never once, with any man?* He did not withdraw, as she had more than half expected him to do. Looking at the acceptance in the preternaturally handsome face gave her courage. She swallowed.

Just once, she answered, and unlocked the door she had buried along with her sexual development, giving to the Outlander the full truth of what had happened to her as she had never, since her brother Teague, at the risk of his life and against the orders of the MasterRank Bard Riordan, had rescued her.

With the queer double sight of the mind-link, she experienced it all again, along with Cormac's reaction, watched the slim, brown-haired figure of herself as a child walking into nightmare.

An Invader attack on her Kindred, the Boar Kindred, had managed to split them in two, with most under the command of their king, Cadell, and the rest scattering to the deep forest, as they usually did so they could regroup when they had shaken off their pursuers. She, along with her parents and her younger brother Ruark, who was at that time just four winters of age, found themselves cut off from the rest. They could not move as quickly as the others, for her mother was heavily pregnant.

"It was just dawn," she said aloud, her tone as dispassionate as she could make it, for the experience through the mind-link was so intense it made her stomach cramp, "and we were on our way to the Spring Gathering, the Bealtuinn.

"Mother and Father, with Ruark and I, were near the end of the line, and we were all bound to trail-silence. The Invaders swept across us with such force and savagery that our resistance was almost impossible to organize. But Cadell did it, and when the fighting disappeared into a haze of dust we knew we must flee.

"Mother was past her time, and old as well for even carrying a child—she had nearly died in the bearing of Ruark. Father took Ruark, and I— all of nine winters old—acted as rearguard for Mother. I'd learned a little of the Power from Teague—who was fostered to the Bards at four winters, so much promise did he have—and I tried to open my mind to the forest so we could decide the best route for escape, but there was too much at hand to worry about. I had my dagger out, watching for Invaders on every front, and we ducked into a deep thicket of brambles. The thorns were so dense that I had to use the dagger to cut a way for Mother and me, though Father and Ruark had gone before us. As we reached the edge of the thicket, I heard Father cry out, and Ruark screamed. When Mother heard Father and Ruark, I could not hold her back. She thrust me aside and went out straight into a band of Invaders. There were six or seven of them, and they caught us all easily. Ruark, being the smallest, wasn't even tied up; an Invader just tossed him over one shoulder while the others tied us together with a thick, harsh cord that passed around our throats as well as our ankles. If one of us fell, or did not walk as they wished, the cord tightened, and we couldn't breathe.

"I don't remember how long we walked, but it was most of the day. They had tied me at the end, so that I could see both Mother and Father. I couldn't see the Invader with Ruark, so I reached for him with my mind. I was a little surprised when he answered, since I'd never tried it before. All I could get from him was that he was alive. I next reached for Father, but he wasn't open, so I tried Mother. That's when I realized she was in labor. When it had started, I never found out, but she was failing by the moment. Soon she would be so far gone that walking would be impossible. I touched her back, and she looked around at me and shook her head, warning me to say nothing. Darkness was beginning to fall, so I hoped the Invaders would stop for the night.

"By the time they did, Mother collapsed where she stood, bringing Father and me down with her. We crawled to her and tried to help her, while the Invaders stood and watched and did nothing. Some of them began to set up camp while the rest of them gathered around us. The one with Ruark came up and dropped him on the ground. He— he's always been quiet, and he just crept up to Mother and took her hand. The whole time, the Invaders talked, and their language is as harsh and guttural and cruel as they were. They laughed and jabbered and pointed, and I hated them with every word and gesture.

"What with the rigors of the fight and the attempted escape and the long walk, Mother hadn't much strength left. None of us were Healer-trained, though we'd seen babies born. I propped her head up on my knee and stroked the hair back from her face. We had no water, no food, nothing. The darker it became, the weaker Mother grew. Then the bleeding began and would not stop. She died in my arms just as the baby was born. It was a boy-child." She swallowed against the dryness in her throat and the sorrow. Quietly, Cormac reached for a wineskin and handed it to her. She drank, grateful for both his thoughtfulness and his continued silence.

"The Invaders untied our bonds long enough to drag Mother's body away," she went on. "They had to hold Ruark down to keep him from following—he was screaming and crying and cursing them, and for once I was glad they didn't speak our language or they would have killed him then and there. I never found out what they did with Mother; dumped her somewhere, I suppose, for they weren't gone long. They tied Father and me back together—once again leaving Ruark free— and forced us to march on to another site, apparently fearing that predators would be drawn to the scent of the blood. Father used his tunic to wrap the baby in, though we had no idea what we would do to feed him.

"Sometime that night, Ruark vanished. We didn't know what had happened to him, whether he had been killed by the Invaders or had run away, forced to the edge of his mental endurance by what he had seen.

"In the morning it was obvious to us that the Invaders had nothing to do with his disappearance. The language they speak, as I said, is a harsh language to begin with, so that they sound angry all the time. They seized Father and shook him and pointed, leaving us in no doubt as to their meaning. Then two of them grabbed me by the shoulders and another took a knife, holding it to my throat. It was appalling. Invaders are enormous men, tremendous fighters, but they rarely bathe, and so they simply reek . . . and sometimes, for all their caution, we could smell them coming. The ones who held me were no exception. I was certain they meant to slit my throat, and between that and their scent, I thought I would vomit. Finally they threw me aside and broke camp. I didn't disgrace myself, somehow, but it was small comfort compared to the worry for Ruark.

"We spent most of the next few days traveling. On the second day the Invaders gave us food—they had allowed us to drink from streams —and we tried to mash up the food for the baby to suck, but he was too weak. He cried and cried until he fell asleep—though we tried to keep him quiet for his own safety—then would awaken and cry some more. On the third day the Invaders took him away, and we never saw him again. I suppose they killed him, too." She saw Cormac close his eyes, then open them again, while the mind-link quivered with his response to her grief.

"Finally we joined up with a larger group of Invaders. I don't remember much about that, because by then the exhaustion and loss had blurred all but the immediate need to survive. Since our capture, Father had turned into an old man. I do remember that they untied us and fastened a metal collar round Father's neck. I suppose I was too young for that; for they didn't put one on me, but put that rope on me again and tied me to Father's collar. Then they took us to a group of other Kindred, guarded by Invaders with whips and clubs. All the adults wore the same collars, with chains between long enough for them to walk without treading on the heels of the one in front. Some of them had children tied to them as well, and every single one—adult and child—bore an attitude of complete indifference. No one would talk to us, and we soon learned why: if you spoke, you were beaten. When Father attempted to speak to them, the guards attacked him. He was a big man and a strong warrior, and when he tried to resist, they beat him until blood ran down his face and back. They finally left him alone when he fell down, unconscious. I did what I could, taking off my tunic and using it to clean him up, but the moon was up before he moved. I didn't look at any of the other Kindred there, though I felt how they wanted to help.

"That first night, our guards went to sleep and the other Kindred gathered around. They told me that resistance was useless; it was best to maintain a completely detached attitude until the guards slept, which they usually did when gathered in such a large pack. Only at night was it possible to communicate.

"Some of them, they said, had been prisoners far longer than we had, and they were from many Kindreds—Hare, Hawk, Stag, to name a few. They helped me with Father, and he soon was able to sit up. But the man I knew was gone. To this day I believe it was because of the blows to his head, for he never spoke again. He looked at me as if he wondered who I was, and from that time onward he was as if a little child.

"I did the best I could with him, and the others gave me what assistance they dared, but he died ten nights later in his sleep. Once again, the Invaders dragged him away.

After that, I—I was alone. As far as I knew, I was the last of my family, save for Teague. Surely Ruark was dead. A child of his age alone in the forest can be easy prey for the creatures who live there, even though reared to its patterns.

"I was tied at the end of the line. With so many prisoners, the Invaders could not move as quickly as they wished. The guards were more alert as we passed through the forest, so we had no more chance to talk between ourselves.

"The Kindred had told me that because of my age, it was probable I would be sold as a pleasure-slave. I didn't know what that meant, and none of them would elaborate. All I got from them was a sense of degradation far beyond our current lot, and though it is not our way to permit fear, I began to be frightened. I knew, somehow, that once we reached the main Invader camp I would be lost." She drank again, feeling her fingers shake on the wineskin. Still Cormac waited, did not touch her, knowing she needed the distance to tell her story. She glanced at him, saw in the faint light the vivid intensity of his blue eyes, and dropped her eyes to her hands.

"But no one came to rescue us, and three moons after the ambush, we arrived at the Invader camp. It was a scene of complete and utter chaos—we found out later that our arrival coincided with the arrival of more than fifty longboats from overseas, so the camp was all but bursting at the seams with Invaders, their household goods, and newly taken Kindred slaves.

"Our group was divided into men, women, and children. The men were led off, then the women. The children remained. I never knew any of the names of my fellows; partially because I was too wrapped up in myself to make an effort to learn anything about them, but more because I wanted to escape—in spite of what we had been told—and knew I could do it better alone, so I remained aloof and unfriendly to their overtures. I would rather make the attempt and die for it than accept slavery blindly.

"The first three or four days of my captivity was spent tied inside a wooden structure. Food and water were brought to us once a day. We found the lack of water a hardship, because we are accustomed to cleanliness. There was scarcely enough water for all of us to drink, let alone wash in. I'm not sure how many of us there were, probably nearly thirty in that little place. We were all younger children—the youngest being around three winters—all the way up to thirteen or fourteen winters. It was filthy, and it stank, and I thought the Invaders meant to keep us there forever.

"Suddenly, on the third day, one of the Invaders brought in a whole pack of their women, who untied us and took us out to where they had set up great tubs of water. We were stripped, dumped in the water, and scrubbed clean, which ought to have made us feel better, save that it was such a shock and so rudely handled. Once clean, we were not given any clothes at all but taken to an open area. In that area was a wooden floor that had somehow been built so that it stood about chest-high to the Invaders. Once again we were tied, this time in a line to a long piece of wood. We were at the front, so as to be seen by all. Below, filling the air with an anticipation I could taste, stood more Invaders than I had ever seen. One of the boys tied up beside me said that we would be sold to the waiting Invaders. I asked him how he knew, and he said he had learned to understand the language a little during his captivity.

"He was right. One by one my fellow prisoners were sold, and their new masters came up and gave over gold and took them away. Then it was my turn. My rope was untied from the wood and I was forced to stand so that I faced the crowd. The Invader at the end of the rope started shouting at the others, and they shouted back, just as they had during the sale of my fellow captives. I wished then that I'd spent my time learning the Invaders' language instead of nursing my hatred and looking for an escape route. I didn't know what was being said, but I could feel the excitement and something more fouling the air. I didn't want to look at them, to see them staring at my body, so I lifted my chin and stared out beyond them to where I could see, not too far away, the glittering sea. I saw the longboats lying out there with the smaller boats they used to land in, and I saw the vastness of the camp. I wondered then if we would ever be able to defeat them and send them back across the sea, as we had always talked about among ourselves at night around the Gathering fires.

"At last an Invader came up, gave a great heavy pouch to my captor, took my rope, and pulled on it, so I understood I was to follow him. How I wished I had my dagger! But even if I had, there was nowhere I could have hidden it. So I followed, with every nerve on edge, wondering exactly what was expected of me.

"The Invader led me to a tent at the farthest edge of the camp, near the forest, then inside, where he tied me up and stood for a long time staring at me. The longer he stared at me the more intolerable became the atmosphere in the tent; now I know enough to call it lust. Then, I was too young. Eventually he pointed to himself and said a word, which I took to be his name, Svein, though I didn't say it back to him. He said it again, but I refused to respond. Instead, I looked out past his red face and long tangled hair and moustache to the sweet sunlit trees. Somehow, I had to get free of this rope, and to do that I needed a knife. Once I had a knife I was as good as free.

"He jerked me to him and began kissing me, his hands roaming down across my body, and the shock of it made me jump with a fear and a horror I'd never experienced. The more I resisted, the more aroused he became, until he finally threw me on the ground and took me with the brutal savagery of a beast, not even bothering to disrobe. When he was finished, he stood up, adjusted his clothes, and walked out, leaving me Lying in a pool of my blood and his seed." Her eyes flew to

Cormac, who had shifted abruptly, but he said nothing. Fury and grief lay naked on his face, and through the mind-link came a kind of enraged agony for her that shook her, disrupting the clean lines of her emotional withdrawal. She watched him grip his beautiful, scarred hands together, saw the knuckles turn white.

"I lay for a long time in shock and pain, until I could force myself to get up," she continued at last, her own hands tightening on the wineskin. "I searched for a way to clean myself, and though I did not have a lot of length on the rope, found a pile of clothes near the main pole of the tent. After I wiped myself clean, I tried to dress myself, but I could not get anything over my head because of that rope, so I rummaged until I found a length of cloth and wrapped it around myself, trying to keep the shudders under control, along with the sure knowledge that he might return at any time. As it turned out, I did not see him again until darkness had fallen.

"I knew, from what I had heard growing up, that though the Invaders wanted us as slaves, they had learned to be wary, for we are quick with knives and other weapons. It was drummed into us from birth that it was better to die rather than live as Invader slaves. Occasionally escaped slaves would pass through our territory while heading for the farther mountains and tell us stories about the cruelty and savagery of the Invaders.

"What I saw while journeying to their base camp bore this out. They lived under a harsh discipline. Men spent all their time fighting, feasting, and lying with women, whether willing or not. They did not permit women to fight, but made them cook and serve . . . food and other needs . . . and oversee all household matters. The Kindred women fascinated the Invaders because most Invader women were built like the men: big and bulky, with enormous breasts and wide hips.

"Looking back on it now, Svein must have been one of the new arrivals and had either not heard the warnings about Kindred slaves or not heeded them. He came back that night and took me again and again, and finally fell asleep. He had not bothered to remove either his clothes or his dagger, and it was a simple matter for me to find it and free myself—and slit his throat. It was agony to move, but I found something to wear and used the knife to hack it off to a length that would not trip me, then huddled at the entrance to the tent until the camp fell quiet.

"Using the shadows, I crept from tent to tent until I was at the edge of the camp. The Invaders had—of course—posted sentries, so I curled into the side of the closest tent until their patrols led them away from me. I dropped down on my stomach and crawled, not daring to look up in case I was seen. I knew that if I was going to die, I would . . . and I almost—I almost was ready to die. But something drove me on, kept my mind blank of all but the need to escape. Somehow the sentries did not find me. I reached the trees, crawled until I thought I was safe, climbed to my feet to run

. . . and someone grabbed me.

"I didn't make a sound, mainly because whoever it was had their hand clamped over my
mouth. I don't think I could have cried out if I
wanted to—the shock had completely robbed me
of breath. My captor swung me around to face him
. . . and it was Teague. We stared at each other in
utter astonishment, and I began to cry. So did he,
and we stood there in the night holding each other
with tears running down our faces." She swallowed, spoke past the hard edge of memory in her
throat.

"It—it was much later," she whispered, "that
I discovered that Ruark had—somehow—made it
to the Bards' training camp, where he found
Teague. Riordan, who was—and is—very close to
Teague, forbade him to look for me. Teague dis-
obeyed and, leaving Ruark with the Bards, tracked
me to the camp. He knew which tent I was in and
was trying to put together a plan to get me out
when I literally ran into him."

Kerensa fell silent, not trying to hide the tears
that slid down her face. All at once she felt exhausted, drained . . . and free. Cormac, reading her,
reached out, pulled her to him, and held her with
wordless tenderness.

"You," he said in a voice so hoarse it was
scarcely audible, "are giving me a greater gift than
I deserve."

She shook her head, unable to speak. *You're the
gift*, she said into the beautiful peace of their mind-
link. She gave him back look for look, letting her

eyes say what words could not. The last of the shadows were gone, vanished like mist in the sun.

With an easiness that almost startled her, she reached for the lacing of his tunic, her fingers shaking so that she could not control them. He shuddered, closed his eyes, and did not move. Their minds were still linked, and she marveled at the give and take, the perfect seamlessness. She had been involved with mind-links all her life, and this one transcended the others, in the same way that a nestbound fledgling cannot truly know the limitless freedom of the soaring hawk until it has dared the air. Each movement of her hands sent a response through him that echoed back into her, so that she wasn't sure who was the more aroused. Slowly he drew off her tunic, then cupped her face, drawing his thumbs down to trace the contours, the outline of her lips.

With a gasp, she caught at his hands, and he stopped, a quizzical line between his brows.

"Cormac" she breathed. "I can't—you make me—"

"Kerensa—" he whispered, his voice husky with the force of his passion. In one fluid motion, he buried his face between her breasts. The sensation rocked her, stole her breath; her arms came around him and held him there. His clean scent, the touch of his skin against hers, and his acceptance all quivered through her with the force of a blow. Her eyes went down seeking his, and he looked up; golden-brown met and held vivid blue. Through the mind-link, she felt his own raw need

. . . his own deep insecurities. He held nothing back; she assimilated it all and sensed how he did the same with her. A peculiar, gentle smile, one she had never before seen, woke on his face and transformed it; she knew it was how he must have looked before the Starsworn had taken him and molded him into the ultimate warrior.

His mouth came down hard on hers and no more words were necessary.

Wild Women Don't Get the Blues

by Nancy Orlando

Wild women don't get the blues. I think about the first time I saw those words, on a bumper sticker, when Savannah was still an infant—I can visualize her in her car seat, plump and blanketed, as we drove uptown on that bitter cold winter morning, the sherbet glow of the sun just poking above the mountains to the east. The words had startled me by the intensity of emotion that they evoked. They had been a bittersweet reminder of times when mountains and rivers were what defined and formed my life—then I had been mired in the domesticity and demands of raising Savannah and longed for something other than diapers and feeding schedules to give my day form.

Savannah is ten now, and I liken raising her to a long, arduous hike on which, more often than not, you see where the path has taken you in retrospect. I feel now that it had taken a combination of naïveté, chutzpah, and hubris for Sam and I even to have had a child. We thought of ourselves as good, kind, and capable people, but at our young ages we had never been tested by adversity, and at the time we conceived Savannah, we had never even articulated our reasons for wanting a child.

Not that Sam would need to. Life, for him, was simply a matter of overcoming inertia, a series of steps to get from one point to another. In many ways, that seems the sanest way of getting through it, but for me life was the cause of what Sam affectionately, I think, called my "existential angst," a certainty that every decision I made had consequences of universal scope. When Savannah was still in the deciding stages, I had an overwhelming inability to reach a decision. Ultimately, I decided by not deciding. I began paying less attention to birth control and more attention to sex. Sam and I both knew we had in some way decided to have a child, as if leaving it unspoken could somehow negate the enormity of our decision.

We were living in Los Angeles then, a place I can see now gave little sustenance, but its energy and intensity seemed important at the time. Sam was working in construction, I in a restaurant, and we thought little of where this was leading us. The balmy warmth juxtaposed with the intensity of L.A. provided a languid energy for our relationship. We lived in an apartment, above an eccentric old woman whose mailbox proclaimed her to be Miss Emmaline Winchester something or other. I referred to her simply as Miss Emma. She had a predilection for incessantly playing old Gershwin tunes on her stereo and for reminiscing a bit too long when we ran into each other at the mailbox. "Run into" really isn't the right term, for I was usually ready to leave when Miss Emma would come shuffling out of her apartment, stale lilac cologne announcing her presence. As we sifted through our mail, I learned to inject the proper "oohs" and "um-hums" at her faded memories without thinking about the actual content of her conversation. Miss Emma was a nice enough landlady, and I listened to her every day as if I were hearing it all for the first time. Often she spoke of what it was to have been young in L.A., but even though I reached into the farthest corners of my imagination, I could barely imagine Miss Emma ever being young.

I think back on those days after Savannah was conceived, and before Sam or anyone else knew, as surreal and dreamy. Letters from home—news of births, deaths, and distant relatives gone mad— were read to the sounds of Miss Emma's Gershwin records seeping up into our apartment. Dusty images were conjured up by hometown news— clapboard houses painted pink or yellow (for that was the style then), my childhood house among them, a bicycle in front and a stubborn bare spot on the lawn. Memories of childhood always as summer. It was during this time that I left Sam. Not really left, but sort of cold-feet abandoned him for a few days.

When I went to work on that morning, Miss Emma's cat was on the stoop, a sentinel of my workday. He was always there when I left for Millie's, the coffee shop where I waited tables. I like to think of that day as the one on which Savannah's life really began. I remember Millie—the owner and my boss—complaining of the heat and blaming it on Russian spacecraft, the cigarette smoke clinging randomly to shafts of light in the corner, distorted images of myself in stainless steel coffee-pots, which boiled over as I listened to customers with sandpaper voices and names like Red, who I supposed once really had red hair and a voice that was young and cooing. Franny Eberhard was there that day, too, drinking her endless cups of coffee and, as always, a magazine photograph of JFK on her table alongside photographs of her sons as young children. Silverware placed neatly on white paper napkins reflecting my sliced image back to me, dried bits of yellow egg yolk on white dinner-ware, red tennis shoes greeting the paunch of a middle-aged man as he walked in, a nervous nauseousness in my stomach—all these memories are still startling in their immediacy.

At the end of that day, instead of returning home I drove north through the labyrinth of the L.A. freeway, which eventually opened up to rolling hills, before straightening out like a ribbon laid flat upon the earth through the San Joaquin Valley. I drove through small farming towns, tilled fields that undulated in furrowed rows, whose color reminded me of coffee-stained white cloth napkins. At Fresno, I turned east toward the mountains. The mountains—where Sam and I had met. Their outline rose from the flatness of the valley. As I passed a mall, I realized how ill-equipped I was and stopped to purchase a sleeping bag, rudimentary camping supplies and proper clothes. The searing heat of Fresno gave way to cooler breezes, which calmed and lulled me up the mountain. I thought of all the times Sam and I had driven this highway, up past orange groves, through hills that rose and fell, draping themselves over boulders and around scrub oak and manzanita, until the oak and manzanita gave way to stunted pines, and then around one curve in the highway the stunted pines gave way to lush, dense lodgepole and redwood.

It was dark and I rolled down the windows, intoxicated by the scent of pine that the surrounding night breeze wrapped around me. I thought of Sam, not yet ready to call him, yet knowing I must. Of course, when I did call him, he had been there—home for me in more than one way. Steady Sam, solid Sam, supporting Sam. All of those things. He later told me he knew then that I was pregnant; he understood me well enough to know that my actions had not been a reaction to him. In fact, he had understood it before me, that my reactions to Savannah's conception had been some sort of intuited maternal thing that my life was changing in ways I could not yet comprehend. Those days away had been rites of passage for the freedom of our life together, the indulgence of unfettered time and fulfillment of only my needs.

Exhausted, I found a campsite and laid my bag under the stars that night and thought about Sam and I here. Taciturn Sam was amused by others who had come to the mountains on some sort of sacred mission. While others I knew had climbed peaks seeking God, or Buddha, or whomever and changed convictions as easily as they did their clothes, Sam stood steadily removed from all that. Even then, I guess, he understood that it was all a matter of overcoming inertia. It took me awhile to understand that in him, and for a long time I resisted his lack of apparent seeking, but in the end he turned out to be just what I needed.

Sleep crept into my body like a silent cat. The night air on my face was accompanied by dreams of Gershwin tunes on my radio, a freckled young man with red hair and a walking stick smiling and dancing through our L.A. apartment, while an infant in a white wicker basket surrounded by fresh lilacs gazed on adoringly, gurgling and smiling at the dancing young man. I awoke to sunlight filtering through the tops of pines, the light softening and blurring the images around me. After a few days, I did return to Sam, where we reveled in the newfound image of ourselves as expectant parents.

It was shortly after that we left L.A. and came to New Mexico, where Sam had lived before. New Mexico was, for Sam, like some long ago but not forgotten lover, a place whose memories offered nurturing and comfort. At first, the grit and brownness of the landscape alienated me, but I was slowly able to abandon the notion of green as a standard for all things wild. The land gave itself to me, tentatively—the skies that at one time had seemed too omnipresent and pressing now felt like a familiar blanket, and I couldn't imagine not having such iridescence above and not being surrounded by the mountains and mesas.

It was here that Savannah was born. Sam was at the birth. My friend Phyllis described childbirth to me as feeling like a Mack truck had driven through you—a description I found humorous but thought exaggerated. After Savannah's birth, however, it became an apt description. At the same time, it was hard to believe how something so painful and messy could have so much power and glory in it. At least that's how it felt to me—I had never liked my body more than in those few days after Savannah was born. I speak of her now as if we always knew her name would be Savannah, but that is not true. At her birth, when she slid out of me,—bloody, warm, mysterious, and musky, I had wanted a strong name, with grace. The images of grasses swaying in the wind, lithe, elegant, and flourishing from the earth was my vision of what I hoped for her—to be strong yet supple and to gain sustenance from where she lived, no matter how harsh the place.

After the first chimerical weeks with Savannah passed, Sam, Savannah, and I settled into what would be a routine for our first year as parents— me caring for Savannah while Sam worked. It hadn't felt like a hard decision for me then to stay with Savannah; moreover, I felt here is a child, my child, who needs to be cared for, and I am her mother. Simple and clear, or so I thought at the time. But once the neediness and routine of caring for Savannah became apparent, the dreamlike quality of Savannah and our first days gave way to a numbness. I often caught myself daydreaming. A line from some poem read long ago about "days running away like wild horses over the hills" kept repeating in my mind. Depending on what sort of day or night it had been with Savannah, I could imagine myself on the horses leaving Savannah and her poop and spit-up and demands behind—running over spring-greened hills on chestnut brown horses, wild and free as the wind. Always fatigued, my brain and body felt soft and pasty like risen bread dough waiting to be punched down.

Our days together took on a torpid simplicity. I judged the temperature outside by how easily the diaper cream slid over Savannah's butt, thinking to myself that I was really smarter than all this, I knew better, I had read all the books, but nobody had written that it would be like this. Mostly too tired to think of life beyond nursing Savannah and sleeping, I lapsed into an inane TV routine. Phil and Oprah in the morning, Geraldo in the afternoon, the foibles of other lives taking on added significance as the scope of mine diminished. Sam came home one day to find me weeping over a rerun of a "thirtysomething" in which Elliot grapples with his lapsed Catholicism. I tried to explain the helplessness I felt to Sam, knowing that I didn't have that kind of religion to offer to Savannah, and how I was afraid of all the love I felt for her, afraid because at times I had wanted to escape the burden of that love.

  Sam and I became divided over such issues— he accusing me of carrying my existential angst too far, and I accusing him of disinterest in Savannah and me. Of course, I know now that this was a dance for only Savannah and me, one with steps for only two. Sam and I had several silent days over that episode, and I countered my rage at him by immersing myself in even more television. I cast myself in imaginary dramas as a salve—chance encounters with former lovers who found my perceptions profound and my body alluring, and who begged me to leave the baneful existence I was leading. But, slowly and subtly, Sam had in my eyes shaped up, and we broke through to each other. Perhaps nothing more really happened than that we finally acknowledged that Savannah had indeed changed what we were to each other, and we had broadened our relationship to make room for her.

It was around this time that I overcame my inability to be out of Savannah's presence and began rising early to swim laps at a nearby pool, letting Sam handle Savannah's early morning cantankerousness. My body shaped up and my mind became clearer, and in spite of the fact that I had risen before the sun to swim and would have to return home in time for Sam to leave for work, I began to enjoy that solitary and rhythmic time. Swimming in the glass-enclosed pool, I watched the sun rise over the mountains to the east. Arm up, down, pulling through water, over and over, water over limbs, limbs pushing through water, I imagined myself the personification of monks chanting, bathed in the holy orange light of the sunrise.

As Savannah grew, my dance with her changed. I began to take time for other things. I started working with clay again—something I had abandoned to the limitations of pregnancy and demands of Savannah's younger years. I threw pots, and when some of the pots began to sell and galleries expressed interest, I could not believe that others would want them, although Sam told me otherwise. To me, they seemed artless and earthbound vessels that I struggled to take beyond mere utility. I tediously labored with form. I became obsessed with curves as representation, connotation, and suggestion of something greater. The curve between Sam's neck and shoulder as we made love, the arc of bare tree limbs against a

winter twilight, the motion of Savannah's arms the
first time she reached for me were images that
filled my mind as I thinned clay walls, pushing and
pulling forms out of cold globs of clay. Sam often
came home in those days to find me laboring with
wet piles of clay or pondering sketches of curves
and lines that I had tacked all over the converted-
garage studio. It was during this time that I began
listening to country music—it seemed to epitomize
musically what I was struggling for in my pots—
emotion stripped to its essence, no cluttering of
sentiment.

Many years later I spoke of these initial days
of motherhood to some friends. In a bar, over beers,
I questioned these other women, some mothers by
childbirth, others through marriage, about whether
they had ever wanted to abandon the insistent
burden of love their children demanded. Some of
my friends stared at me as if I were Mommy Dear-
est incarnate, but in one or two I saw a glimmer of
understanding, a recognition of words for their
experience, a relief at the articulation of feeling. I
wondered what it was that had kept us from giving ourselves over to the overwhelming banality
of those early days with our children and considered us to be faith substantiated.

I was often surprised at the intensity of rage
that Savannah was capable of eliciting in me. Rage,
when she was an infant and I was incapable of
comforting her—an affront to my role in her life.
Rage, in later years at what I saw in Savannah as
a poor reflection of me—things I had hoped to

impart to her, mirrored back as a distorted version
of myself. Sam always told me at those times that
I was too hard on myself, and I can understand
now that it was an error to project so much of
myself onto Savannah. On the sweet side of that
rage was Savannah's ability to remind me of all
that was good between Sam and me. When we
were in a place where it was difficult to feel the
grace of our marriage, Sam's strength and kindness
with Savannah could show me what I could not
see on my own.

I often told Savannah I loved her, and she, me.
How free and easy it was for Savannah and I to
exchange "I love you." I wanted Savannah to take
these words as a shield against the inevitable dif-
ficulties of growing up, and imagined the nuances
that those same words would take on as she grew
older. "I love you," so don't ride your bike wildly
through traffic as soon as you leave my sight. "I
love you," so choose a boyfriend, husband, or lover
I will approve of. "I love you," so realize yourself
in ways that I can understand. "I love you," so do
not forget that I am your mother. I wished for
Savannah that "I love you" could remain as pure
and real as in her childhood, but I knew that was
not possible. I wondered how we adults could
convolute words so essential, and remembered
Savannah at five, she and a friend dancing freely
to the words of some country song, arms swaying
and mouths upturned to the sky. Poignant and
bittersweet, their innocence was magnified by the
sorrow of the song—words of good love gone bad,

innocence lost.

We took Savannah to the mountains often, Sam and I. She had hiked with us as an infant, hunkered down on our backs in a baby carrier and, as she grew older, on her own. Sam had taught her to fish, and I would watch her and Sam examining the stomach contents of a dead trout, deciding what to use as bait. In the morning we would watch the mists burn off the river, Sam, Savannah and I, crouched over a fire, my hands cupped around the warmth of a mug, absently fingering the throwing marks and indentations the potter had left on it.

I thought about our reasons for going to the mountains and hoped we were giving Savannah a connection to something essential. I thought of what Savannah had given me—my mortality, a boundary and urgency to my life. I often took my bike up to the mountains, riding a steep trail that formed a canyon above the foaming white ribbon of a river that undulated and beckoned far below. The scent of the willows pummeled my face while I glided down the trail, tires spitting gravel out behind me, my hands gripping the handlebars. The play of sunlight and shadow on the road rippled into a blur, a strobe pattern of light and dark as I sped down the trail.

Overcoming inertia, simple yet so hard. One foot in front of the other. You get out of bed in the morning, or you don't. You place one foot in front of the other, or you don t. You open your eyes, or you don't. You see the sunset, listen for the breeze in the trees, the silence of snow, or you don't. To find the sacred in the mundane. I think of Savannah. Savannah at three, telling me the sun had melted at sunset. Savannah at five, telling me that the wind in the trees is the sound of God. And knowing these memories will always be, I smile. Wild women don't get the blues.

Come September

by Donna Stuart

M ama shuffles through a pile of Sunday newspaper ads and last week's junk mail, sitting on top of the clothes that need mending, sitting on top of the sewing machine. She spills some of the pile off the side.

"Anybody seen that catalog I was looking at?" she hollers, even though I'm right beside her and I'm the only one in the house. I heard Daddy tell Big Mommy (that's his grandma) that Mama's been real distracted lately, worried about bills and stuff, ever since she lost her job with old Doc Somers. Keeled over dead, he did, with a heart attack—right in front of a patient.

"Mama! Watch it!" I squeal as she steps backwards, barely missing the huge poster I'm working on to cover my bedroom door. I've drawn a big red circle, and in the center, I'm working on a portrait of my brother, Charley. When I'm done, I'm gonna put a red line through the circle over his face and below the circle write, "No Charleys Allowed."

Stooping to pick up the battered envelopes and colorful brochures, Mama gives me the usual grunts of dismay. Every little bit she pauses to look over the latest in water softening, encyclopedias, and home video clubs. "Just had it not more than ten minutes ago. I don't know what happens to things anyway," she complains, stepping carefully over me and my markers. "Ever since I had you kids, things just seem to up and walk away."

As if Charley and I have some sort of magical gift for making things disappear.

Leaning into the kitchen doorway, she glares at me and pokes her burgundy-framed glasses to the top of her nose. I decide to make Charley's hair spiked and green. Maybe Mama just needs a new pair of glasses. "You look on the back of the toilet?" I ask her finally. There's always a good pile of stuff there.

What Daddy calls Mama's well-endowed chest rises under her red knit tank top as she sighs and walks toward the bathroom. Returning empty-handed, she shakes her head wearily. "I guess it'll turn up 'fore the day's over. Don't know what to do about this vacuum cleaner business anyway."

Mama broke the vacuum cleaner three weeks ago, Saturday. Big Mommy was on her way to visit and Mama was rushing around clearing away the piles and spraying that lemony stuff all over everything. When she turned the vacuum on, it started making this loud snap, crackle, pop noise like it does when it eats one of Charley's Legos, only worse, like maybe it had choked to death on one.

Snapping the sweeper off, Mama hurried to the door and hollered outside for Daddy. He was in the garage working on Old Man Quincy's car, but when Mama hollers like that, he drops everything and bolts to the door like he's two days late for supper. While Mama scurried around the house with window cleaner, he took one of his screwdrivers to the sweeper. "No use," he told her, "The thing's gone."

"Oh lord," Mama whined. "First Doc Somers and now my only vacuum cleaner. What on earth am I gonna do? Just look at this place. Nothin' but a filthy mess. Big Mommy's gonna think we live in a pigsty." She put her free hand on her hip and pointed the bottle of window cleaner at Daddy like it was gun. "Put it back together," she ordered. "I'm just gonna have to use it that way."

Under his breath, Daddy mumbled something I can't repeat, but started putting the sweeper back together. Mama grunted and dashed to the bathroom to shine the faucets.

As it turned out, Mama couldn't use it that way. The vibrating made her hand numb and the noise gave her a headache. And sure enough, when Big Mommy got there, she took one look at the floor and asked whether or not we enjoyed living like pigs.

Finally, Mama gives up looking for the mislaid catalog, which advertises vacuum cleaners at the lowest prices of the year. Instead, she goes to the refrigerator and opens the door.

"Can I have some?" I lay down my marker, turning my attention to the open door to see what she takes—usually something tasty when she's discouraged.

"Not gonna eat anything," she insists over her shoulder, letting the door swing shut. "Nothin' good in the house anyway." Like a guard, she leans against the fridge and watches as Daddy, in his old black work boots and dingy green coveralls, walks in. He sits a silver lunch pail on the counter.

"Any leftovers?" I say to Daddy. This is my last chance before supper.

"Naw." He clops over to give Mama a peck on the cheek, then tucks some of her wavy blond hair back into place. "You oughta wear your hair down, sugar. Anybody who has hair the color of vanilla ice cream oughta display it properly."

Mama grunts, as if she's annoyed, but lets him nuzzle her neck for longer than I care to say. I change positions, for a better angle, so I can make one of Charley's teeth black as coal.

"Go get cleaned up." She pushes his grimy

hands away, but smiles all the while, "supper be ready pretty soon." He pulls out a chair, sitting down to unlace his boots. Now, Mama's not too fussy about piles, but sure as you wear shoes on her carpet, she'll give you all kinds of grief.

Mama stirs the pot of dumplings simmering on the stove. "Anybody seen Charley?" she says into the black kettle, then blows on a moist, hot, yellow dumpling and takes a nibble out of its side.

"In the tree house." Daddy tosses a boot into the pantry, watching Mama like he's near hypnotized.

Between nibbles, she looks at him and raises her eyebrows, "You gonna be late for supper, you don't get a move on."

I better hurry, too, I tell myself, before Charley comes in and ruins my poster, then I dot his face with ugly brown warts, the finishing touch. As I hang it on the outside of my bedroom door, I hear Mama calling everybody to eat.

"Char-ley," she hollers and the back door claps. Then she comes to the bottom of the stairs. "Ker-mit. Sep-tem-ber." That's Daddy and me. Mama named me September because she and Daddy and I all have birthdays in September. Charley came along and ruined everything by being born on August twenty-eighth. "Sup-per's rea-dy."

Daddy used to hate his name, till I told him about Kermit the frog. One day, when Mama was giving him a hard time about it, I said to him, "Daddy, you ain't got nothin' to be ashamed of.

Why, there's even a famous frog who has your name."

"Is that right, Princess?" Daddy grabbed me and swung me around the room till we both had to hold on to the counter to stand up straight. Then he said, "I believe this is cause for celebration," and told us to get our shoes on, we were going to Dairy Delight for supper.

He's put on a few extra pounds since old Doc Somers croaked and Mama's been home, cooking all his favorite foods. But his very favorite is chicken and dumplings, so unlike most nights, it takes no time at all for him to get to the table. Even so, I believe Mama looks slightly dismayed at the lost chance to complain about his tardiness.

Mama leans across the table and dips out a serving of dumplings for Charley. He moans something about pizza, stacking his arms across his chest. Daddy scolds him for not appreciating Mama's effort. Mama looks pleased as a peacock and says, "See there, Charley, not everybody's like *you*. Some people appreciate good home cooking." Then she leans toward Daddy and dips out his portion, too, something she never, ever does. Now Daddy's the one who looks pleased.

I know better, but the temptation is too much. "Yeah, Charley, some of us appreciate Mama's cooking." He sticks his tongue out at me, inviting me to give him a good wallop under the table.

"September," Mama scolds, "that'll be enough already." I squirm in my chair a bit and look down at the yellow lumps on my plate and pick up my napkin and lay it across my lap. Mama says it's real important to use good manners.

Finally, she sits down, pulling her right leg up under her bottom, pouring tea over a tall glass of ice. Daddy tells her how scrumptious the dumplings are. She smiles at him and says, "Why, thank you, Kermit," like it's the nicest thing anybody's ever said to her.

After our plates are about half-empty, Mama reaches up and winds her stray hairs around a finger, then twists sideways in her chair. "New catalog came today," she says, as casually as possible for somebody who's got something up her sleeve.

Daddy frowns. The picture's coming into focus now and he doesn't like what he sees. Every time Mama cooks dumplings and starts talking about catalogs, we all know she's got it in her head to buy something.

"It did, did it?" he says through his napkin, wiping yellow gravy off the side of his thick, reddish-blond moustache.

"Yeah," she says slowly, eyes glued to the dumpling on her fork. "Got some real nice vacuum cleaners on sale. One in particular I'm thinking of. On closeout for one hundred forty-nine dollars and ninety-nine cents." She puts the dumpling in her mouth and chews, pushing another in circles around her plate.

"Now, Sue Ellen." Daddy puts his napkin down. Mama ignores him and as soon as her mouth is empty—she'd never talk with it full—

rambles right on.

"That's a whole hundred dollars off its regular price. 'Course," she goes on dreamily, her chin perched on the heel of her hand while she waves the empty fork in the air, "you should see some of those vacuum cleaners. Why, there's one for three hundred ninety-nine dollars and ninety-nine cents—*on sale*. Has all kinds of attachments and settings. One for the stairs. One for the furniture. One for the curtains and lamp shades. Why, the thing even has a shampooer and is self-propelled. Now, what do you think about that?"

Daddy shakes his head in slow motion. "I don't see how, Sue Ellen. I thought we settled this already. Come September, when the new doc gets here and you get back to work, then we can go invest in a new sweeper."

Charley and I sit real still, staring at what's left of our yellow lumps. I feel like I'm about a foot away from Big Mommy's old pressure cooker, clattering on the stove, ready to blow up all over me at one wrong touch.

"Maybe I changed my mind." Mama sits up in her chair, stiff as an ax. "And don't you tell me, Kermit Slone, whether or not I can get a new sweeper. If I want a new sweeper, I'll have a new sweeper."

Without moving my head, I steal a peek at Daddy. " 'Course you will, sugar," he says calmly, but I see panic in those eyes. And now, he's said the worst possible thing. "Patronizing her," Mama calls it, but I know, like me, he's remembering two summers ago when the mid-summer sale catalog came, and Mama got it in her head to have a swimming pool—one on closeout for one hundred forty-nine dollars and ninety-nine cents.

It was the hottest summer I ever remember, even though, as Mama says, I am *only* a child. June Kitchen, who lives in town, bought a new pool and invited everybody over for a party. Mama splashed and laughed and said she'd never felt so refreshed in her entire life.

Now our yard isn't flat and clear like the Kitchels'. It goes up the side of Poke Mountain and has a lot of nice old trees. Daddy told Mama our yard wasn't suited for a swimming pool, but Mama insisted there was room for a small one, a one hundred forty-nine dollar and ninety-nine cent one.

So after work one Saturday, Mama and me and Charley drove more than an hour to the mall. Mama marched into the store and asked for someone to direct us to the swimming pool department. After she spoke to the saleslady, she turned and asked me and Charley if we thought three and a half feet deep and fifteen feet around would be too big for our yard—seems they just sold the last one for one hundred forty-nine, ninety-nine. And we'd driven an hour, after all.

Charley and I giggled and nodded our approval and asked Mama to buy us fluorescent green goggles and an alligator float. She smiled, like we were all getting away with murder, and said, "might as well go ahead," as she handed the saleslady her charge card. Then they loaded the pool in the back of our four-by-four and Mama drove it home to Daddy.

Frowning and wiping his hands on an old rag, he came out of the garage. Mama just looked at him and said, "Put it together, Kermit."

Daddy sighed and slid out the box. Shaking his head, he mumbled something about the things Mama gets him into, then stacked everything beside the garage. Wiping the sweat from his forehead, he turned to me and Charley. "I swear I don't know what this heat has done to your Mama's brain."

Mama grunted at him, then stomped into the house for some iced tea. Daddy spent all his free time for the next two weeks trying to level a place in the backyard where he could set up the pool. Then Charley and I had a big party, like the Kitchens'. Only, a couple of Charley's friends brought pistols that shoot tiny yellow balls. Yes, sir, and that's what they did. I bet they shot fifty of them into the pool.

Mama took the net the saleslady told her she needed to keep the water clean and tried to get them all out, cursing Kyle Raimey and Brett James all the while, but Daddy had to keep taking the jammed filter apart to remove tiny yellow balls.

Next thing you know, some of the trees out there start shedding these hard brown things. Bless her heart, Mama kept making her rounds with that net, useless as it was. Daddy finally hung a little tool box, like a birdhouse, on the side of tree next to what he'd come to call the Time Sucking Machine.

In the spring, Mama ran an ad and sold the pool to a man who wanted one for his grandchildren. He was supposed to take it down himself, sparing Daddy the trouble, but when Mama uncovered the water, it was putrid—that's what she called it, *putrid*. Just the sound of it makes you want to hold your nose. And the liner was stained. She and Daddy tore the pool apart, then gave the man a hundred dollars of his money back to go buy a new liner.

Grandpa bumped his way out our drive, with the timesucking machine in the back of his truck, and Daddy put his arm around Mama. She leaned her head over on his shoulder and muttered something about learning lessons the hard way.

In a huff now, Mama stands up and stomps over to the counter where she fills a bowl with ice cream, then stomps into the family room. I hear her pop on the television. Jeanetta Wiley is talking about sunshine for the rest of the week.

Gathering the courage to look up from my plate again, I find Daddy grinning and I'm totally confused. With his pointy finger practically stuck up his nose, he shushes me and Charley, then grabs his red cap off the refrigerator. He's pinned Mama's black shoulder pads to it so it looks likes a giant Mickey Mouse hat.

He motions for us to follow him into the pantry. Standing on his tippy toes, he reaches up on the very top shelf, behind the Christmas ham roasting pot, to pull out our chipmunk jar, which used to hold peanut butter, but now holds our Special Fund. I start to protest but he shushes me again.

"September," he says quietly. "Charley." Now, I'm sorry, but with that hat on, I have a hard time taking this man seriously. "You all are gettin' old enough to learn somethin' about priorities." He clears his throat. "Obviously gettin' a new vacuum cleaner is very important to your Mama. As you heard, she's not content to wait till September. So I feel, since she does so much to contribute to the well-being of our family and all, we should take the money from our Special Fund and purchase her that new sweeper. Besides, it wouldn't do for a family who couldn't afford to replace their sweeper to go to Disneyworld, would it? That's what I mean about priorities, deciding what's most important for our well-being."

"But Daddy," I whine, bouncing up and down to be convincing, "if we do that, we'll never get to go." Our Fund is three years old, and has one thousand (yes, I said, *one thousand*), three hundred, thirty-six dollars and twenty-two cents in it, on last count, which was over two months ago. "And besides," I say, "Mama can't even find that catalog with the vacuum cleaners in it."

"Yeah," Charley says, "Why can't Mama keep borrowing Big Mommy's sweeper?"

"You-all know how your Mama feels about borrowin' things. Only thing she hates worse than borrowin' is being late somewheres." That's true, I think, and all the times I've had to spend waiting with Charley in the backseat 'cause we're half an hour early flash through my head. Suddenly, I see black bars across the windows of our four-by-four and I'm chained to Charley, waiting for Big Mommy to get home so we can borrow her sweeper.

I look up at what Mama calls Daddy's puppy-dog eyes and I figure he's probably worried about what lesson Mama might have to learn the hard way if we don't do this.

"Okay," I force through gritted teeth.

"Okay," Charley says, too.

"Stop mockin' me." I jab him in the side with my elbow.

"I'm not mockin' you." He steps on my foot with his heel.

"Are to." I smack him across the belly with the back of my hand.

"Are not." And before he can smack me, Daddy reaches his thick, hairy arm down between us.

"Enough, you fellers." Daddy pushes Charley out of my reach.

"At the end of the week, Mama has to go to the office to meet the new doc and arrange to work for him when he takes over in September. We'll go to the mall and pick up the vacuum cleaner then, but I want to surprise her, so you-all keep your traps shut, you hear?"

"Okay, Daddy, but how will we know which one to get?"

"Okay, Daddy, but how will we know which

one to get?" Charlie sticks his tongue out at me again. I try to smack it down his throat, but Daddy catches my arm before it reaches Charley's face.

"The one for one hundred forty-nine dollars and ninety-nine cents. The one that's one hundred dollars off its regular price," says Daddy, as if it's simple as two plus two. "But you-all better be quiet about it, now, or I swear, I'll never forgive you."

Daddy unscrews the chipmunk's blue lid and counts out one hundred sixty dollars. I clutch the shelf with my hand—I think I'm gonna be sick. One hundred sixty dollars for a vacuum cleaner. Then I see it, clear as the freckles on my face, Mama's new sweeper sucking up my airline ticket to Florida.

"This'll do it, tax and all."

"I should certainly hope so," I say.

"I should certainly hope so," mimics Charley, who trips over my foot as we come out of the pantry. Mama walks into the kitchen, giving us her most hateful look. Seems she's going over to Big Mommy's to borrow the sweeper so she won't be helping us clean up the kitchen. After she's gone, Daddy tells us she likes to make her point.

While Daddy and Charley work on the dishes, he puts me to work finding the missing catalog so we know exactly what it is we're going after. I have a slight advantage, knowing the places Mama has already looked. It doesn't take long. I don't know why, but I seem to have a knack for turning up what's missing.

Sure enough, behind the buffet, I find the

missing catalog, along with eight cents (one hundred, fifty-nine dollars, and ninety-two cents left to replace), Charley's crumpled coloring book, my missing Barbie doll's head, and a pair of underwear (I won't say whose). There are also those little things called dust bunnies, which I'm certain Mama will take care of once she gets her new sweeper.

On Friday morning Mama is still sulking over the missing catalog and close-out sweeper. I figure it's a good thing we're going to the mall today or who knows what might happen. I watch as she puts on her best clothes and fusses over her makeup.

Doc Adams is just out of med school. Mama tells me she went to high school with his older brother, but not that much older. Says the doc was always causing mischief and getting into trouble. "Sounds like Charley," I grumble, and she smiles into the mirror like she knows something I don't.

Pulling her beautiful blond hair back, she braids it, and I wonder why she doesn't leave it down—displaying it properly, like Daddy says, for the new doc. While she works at it, she tells me she thinks Daddy hid the catalog. Unlike turning up mislaid objects, I am not too good at keeping secrets.

"And furthermore, I do not understand why he has insisted on stayin' home with you kids today. He knows how much you like to go up to Big Mommy's to play with Lizzy's kids."

"Don't know." I tumble off her bed. "Don't

know nothin' 'bout nothin'."

"I smell a skunk," Mama sings.

I make a mad dash for the door.

When we get home later, Mama is back in her shorts and tank top. Stretched out on the porch swing, she flips through one of her women's magazines and sips iced tea. Thank goodness it's not a catalog, I think, and wish I had bought one of those combination locks for the chipmunk jar.

Daddy follows me and Charley up the front steps and goes over to give her a peck on the cheek. "How'd everything go?"

"Just fine. He'll be openin' the office Tuesday after Labor Day. I'm all set to go back to work." She swings her feet to the floor, sitting up. "Where you-all been anyway?"

"Why don't you come out here and see?" Daddy grabs her by the hand, tugging her off the swing.

"What's going on?" She lowers her voice, grinning like a silly old goose. "My birthday won't be here till September."

"We know," I say, following them down the steps.

"We know," says Charley, out of my reach, so the most I can manage is an evil eye.

Daddy lifts up the door to the four-by-four, grinning like a school boy, pointing at the new sweeper. "This is where we've been."

"You-all," Mama says, her voice still two octaves lower than normal. She plants a big kiss right below his moustache He grabs her around the

waist and she bends her knees, pulling her feet up
behind her, then he swings her in circles. Just like
he did me. She kisses him a hundred million times
all over his face and keeps saying, "I don't believe
you-all."

When Daddy deposits her back on solid
ground, both of them stagger and smooth their
clothes and hair like they just came off a ride at
the amusement park. "I knew you were up to
somethin'," Mama says, stumbling over her fingers
as she brushes strands of hair away from her
mouth, "but never in a million years did I dream
you'd do this.

"Oh lord." She suddenly eyes us like we're
some sort of criminals. Cocking her head, she
hooks a hand on her hip. "Where did you get the
money? You didn't borrow it from Big Mommy, did
you?"

"The chipmunk jar," squeals Charley. "The
Special Fund. Daddy got it."

"Now, Sue Ellen," Daddy starts before she can
protest. "We all agreed." Daddy pats Charley on
the head.

"You really shouldn't have. I was gonna wait
till September."

And suddenly, there it is again—her new
sweeper sucking up my airline ticket to Disneyworld. "We could take it back," I say somberly.

"September, what a rude thing to say," Daddy
scolds me, which he hardly ever does.

I look up at his puppy-dog eyes. "Sorry,
Daddy."

"Don't tell me you're sorry, young lady. Better tell your Mama."

"I'm sorry, Mama. Really, I am." I stir some gravel with my well-worn sneaker and swat at the tear sneaking down my cheek. "I don't know what got into me."

"It's okay, honey." Mama strokes my hair, which Daddy says is the color of strawberry ice cream—his very favorite. "I understand."

I look up into her pretty blue eyes and forgiving smile and I believe she does. Understand, that is.

As I rub my damp face, Mama puts her arm around my shoulders, giving me a comforting squeeze. "Well," she says to Daddy, "what are you waiting for? Put it together, Kermit."

Daddy winks at me, then shrugs and grrrdips like a big bullfrog.

We all crack up laughing. Even Charley.